"There's a drive in me that has to
work hard at gymnastics. I really want
to do it . . . more than anything."

Tracee trains under three-time Olympian gymnast, Linda Metheny, at the National Academy
of Artistic Gymnastics in Oregon, 600 miles
away from her home. She and her teammates
spend seven hours a day, six days a week improving their tricks and routines. They work to
increase their strength and flexibility, master
more difficult tricks, and polish every move for
competition.

"Gymnastics has few heroes.
But Tracee, who is so young, very
extraordinary and ageless in her ability
is, I think, destined to be one."
—*International Gymnast*

The Story of a Young Gymnast

TRACEE TALAVERA

Text and photographs by

Karen Folger Jacobs

BANTAM BOOKS
TORONTO · NEW YORK · LONDON

Christmas
2024 Petra

Enjoy
gymnastics
and
reading
about
Tracee

Talavera

Karen
Folger Jacobs

THE STORY OF A YOUNG GYMNAST—
TRACEE TALAVERA

A Bantam Book / August 1980

Cover photographs copyright by Rafael Beer
Inside photographs, unless otherwise noted, by the author.
Book designed by Lurelle Cheverie

ISBN 0-553-14134-1

Published simultaneously in the United States and Canada

Bantam Books are published by Bantam Books, Inc.
Its trademark, consisting of the words "Bantam
Books" and the portrayal of a bantam, is Registered
in U.S. Patent and Trademark Office and in other
countries. Marca Registrada. Bantam Books, Inc.
666 Fifth Avenue, New York, New York 10103

PRINTED IN THE UNITED STATES OF AMERICA

0 9 8 7 6 5 4 3 2 1

Acknowledgments

Most of all I want to express my deep gratitude to the Talavera family. They shared with me their knowledge and experiences in gymnastics. They welcomed me into their home and lives. During our shared hours I have grown to appreciate the whole Talavera family, the family which created and nurtured someone as tough and sensitive as Tracee.

I would like to extend my thanks to her four coaches, Dick Mulvihill, Linda Metheny Mulvihill, Art Maddox and Mizo Mizoguchi. They were hospitable on my trips to Oregon; they allowed me to watch hundreds of hours of training; and they answered my many, many questions.

There are many other people in the gymnastics world who helped me learn about the sport. I would like to thank them all—especially Marlene Bene of the U.S. Gymnastics Federation, Glen Sunby and Rich Keeney of the *International Gymnast,* Bob Paul of the U.S. Olympic Committee, Hal Frey and Chuck Keeney who coach men's gymnastics at the University of California at Berkeley and Dave Green who coaches the best American tumbling team, Flip City in Newark.

Several people helped me with the photography. In the Oregon gym I had the photographic advice of Art Maddox who was in the sport before Tracee was born. For suggestions in selecting the pictures I thank Joyce Abrams, Bob Charlton, and David Fukuyama.

I am grateful for the prints done by a fine photographer, Margretta Mitchell.

Finally I would like to thank the coaches who taught me gymnastics—Lisa Barber at BART, Bay Area Rapid Tumblers; Mary Dwyer, Lucy Mertz and John Henry Hurtt at the Berkeley YMCA; and Dawn Martin and Dan Millman at the University of California at Berkeley. From them I learned to move my body new ways and to sense mastery of some simple tricks. I enjoyed learning elementary gymnastics.

Foreword

Gymnastics has been a real challenge to me. I work hard at perfecting my gymnastic skills. I like competition and competing—seeing how I do compared to all the other girls in the state, the nation, or whatever.

My advice to gymnasts is to try to be the best gymnast you want to be. And, no matter what level you are, have fun!

T.T.

Contents

The Story
of a
Young
Gymnast

TRACEE
TALAVERA

TRACEE GETS INTO GYMNASTICS

SAN FRANCISCO

When Tracee Talavera was 1½ years old, her parents, Nancy and Rip, received phone calls every night from the woman who lived in the apartment below; she wanted them to stop their daughter from jumping so loudly. Nancy and Rip would check the bedroom. Every time, four-year-old Coral was asleep in her bed, but the crib next to it shook rhythmically in the darkness. In it, smiling Tracee bounced up and down.

The parents would sing or rock Tracee back to sleep, but often the neighbor would call back within the hour. Nancy remembers, "We never told her it wasn't Coral. Who would believe a baby could jump like that? Tracee was hyperactive from birth."

That same year, 1967, a child was "discovered" in a Romanian playground. When coaches Marta and Bela Karoli invited her to train at their gym every day; the girl's parents were relieved. They had replaced their couch four times; six-year-old Nadia Comaneci had broken every one with her nonstop jumping.

Tracee's first gymnastics notebook for acrobatics classes. Taped to the inside cover

2

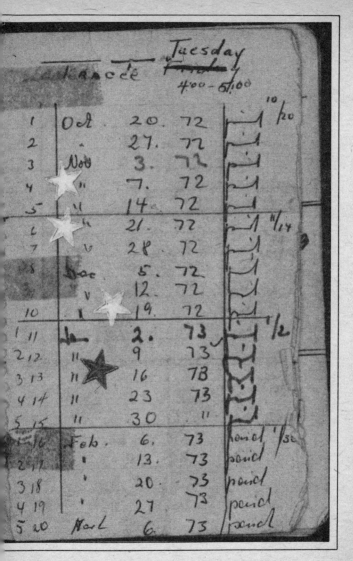

		Tuesday			
	Entrance	4:00 - 5:00			
1	Oct.	20.	72		10/20
2	"	27.	72		
3	Nov	3.	72		
4	"	7.	72		
5	"	14.	72		
6	"	21.	72		11/14
7	"	28.	72		
8	Dec.	5.	72		
9	"	12.	72		
10	"	19.	72		
1 11	Jan	2.	73		1/2
2 12	"	9	73		
3 13	"	16	73		
4 14	"	23	73		
5 15	"	30	"		
1 16	Feb.	6.	73	pencil	1/30
2 17	"	13.	73	pencil	
3 18	"	20.	73	pencil	
4 19	"	27	73	pencil	
5 20	Mar	6.	73	pencil	

is her heroine. The gold stars are for days she did very well. (Photo by William Littlehales)

3

In 1972, Tracee, age five and a half, and Coral, age eight, watched the Olympics on television. Along with millions around the world, they fell in love with Olga Korbut. When the Olympics were over Coral told her parents, "I *have* to learn to do what Olga did!" And Tracee added, "Yeah, we *have* to!"

Nancy and Rip looked for gymnastics classes. But in 1972 nobody in San Francisco taught children's gymnastics. However, they eventually heard of a one-hour acrobatics class held on Tuesdays at a ballet studio.

Nancy helped her daughters keep notebooks, records of each gymnastics class. On days when a student did very well, the teacher glued a gold star next to the date. Inside the front cover of her notebook, Tracee taped a newspaper photo of her heroine, Olga. In these acrobatics classes the sisters did basic rolls, headstands, handstands, and cartwheels.

"We had fun!" Tracee said. "Once the teacher put us in a show. I was wearing a Mickey Mouse costume with a mask and big ears. I had to do a whole bunch of tricks in a circle. I did the tricks okay but the mask moved so I couldn't see out the eye holes. I kept doing the tricks but I crashed into the wall at the back of the stage. It mashed up one mouse ear."

Nancy encouraged her daughters to take ballet lessons along with the acrobatics classes; her sister Shirley danced with San Francisco Ballet Company. Coral and Tracee tried a class, but the ballet teacher did not appreciate them: they practiced cartwheels between ballet steps. Later Tracee told Nancy, "Ballet is too boring! We like to move around more. And

Tracee 6½ and Coral 9, stretch at home in June 1973. (Photo by Nancy Talavera)

Tracee, 7, demonstrates on a trampoline
in a San Francisco park. (Photo
courtesy of San Francisco Chronicle.)

acrobatics isn't hard enough. Mom, we want *real gymnastics.*"

Rip did some investigating and learned that free trampoline lessons were offered near where he and Nancy were raised, and where their parents still live. On week nights and Saturday mornings, Larry "Mac" McNesbitt, a truckdriver, holds his classes in an old building in a city park. Mac has coached there, in the high-ceilinged trampoline room, for forty years. On the wall hangs a poster-size blowup of a 1974 photograph from the *San Francisco Chronicle*. Whenever one of his students lags, he touches the picture and says, to inspire:

"See this? It's seven-year-old Tracee Talavera! I'm so proud to have had a part in training her. Tracee and her big sister, Coral, used to come to all my classes with their father. They were great kids. Coral had beautiful form; she was far superior to Tracee physically. She had great leg strength so she could jump higher and do more difficult tricks than Tracee could. Tracee was always trying to catch up with her sister."

Was there rivalry between the sisters? Mac recalled: "Frankly, I think it helped Tracee. She had somebody to look up to, somebody to model herself on. And Tracee always had a good time in the gym, was always laughing. She seemed so happy-go-lucky, so lovable. But underneath she was a powerhouse, motivation-plus. Tremendous energy."

After Saturday trampoline classes Rip would take his daughters to his parents' home. There the girls would tumble in the backyard. Rafael, 5'2", and known in the family as "Big Rip," decided to make something special for his gymnastics-crazed grand-

Tracee, 7, proudly displays ribbons from her first meet. She scored 7.35 on vault, 6.75 on bars, 5.25 on beam and 5.45 on floor. (Photo by Nancy Talavera)

daughters. One Saturday they arrived to find his present for them—a balance beam. From then on, they spent every Sunday out on that beam until dark. And during the week they would often go to their grandparents' after school to practice on the homemade beam.

After a year of acrobatics, trampolining, and backyard balancing, Coral and Tracee were still pleading for "real" gymnastics lessons. At ages nine and six and a half, they realized that they needed to train seriously to be able to do what Olga did.

Rip and Nancy found that the nearest gymnastics class was held in a town fifteen miles south of San Francisco. Twice a week the family went there, and soon Coral and Tracee were competing in Class III meets, the lowest level of competitive gymnastics.

The whole family began to get more interested in the sport—they read about it, talked about it, and they went to watch Diane Dunbar, the only Elite (highest competitive level) gymnast in northern California. Diane had trained in Walnut Creek, twenty miles east of San Francisco.

WALNUT CREEK

The Talaveras moved to Walnut Creek so that the girls could train with Diane's coach, Jim Gault. (Rip already commuted to the east side of the Bay, to teach at Laney Community College in Oakland.) From San Francisco came the family belongings, including their largest and most expensive piece of furniture—the living-room balance beam.

After enrolling in the local elementary school,

where Tracee was placed in a special class for MGMs (mentally gifted minors), Tracee and Coral began working out at Gault's Diablo Gym Club four afternoons a week. On Sundays the family visited the grandparents; there the girls continued their practice on the homemade backyard beam.

At the Diablo club the Talavera girls learned many new gymnastic tricks and continued to train for competitive events. Six months after Coral entered her first Class II meet, she won the district championship and had her picture in the paper.

During their first summer in Walnut Creek, 1975, the Talaveras took a two-week vacation to Eugene, Oregon, so that the girls could participate in the summer training program of the National Academy of Artistic Gymnastics. All year Coral and Tracee had admired the Academy competitors at meets—especially Leslie Pyfer and Amy Machamer, both of whom were just a year older than Coral. The Talavera sisters wanted to train under their coaches, Dick Mulvihill and Linda Metheny Mulvihill.

For two weeks, every morning Nancy and Rip drove their daughters to the Academy and watched them train with much more advanced gymnasts. Then, at one of the meets, the Talaveras met Gordon Maddox, the gymnast-turned-coach-turned-TV-commentator, "the voice of gymnastics in America" who documented the 1972 Olympics telecast that starred Olga Korbut. He told the Talaveras that one of the finest coaches in the world had just moved from Japan to their area. Mas Watanabe had come to assist Hal Frey, coach of men's gymnastics at the University of California at Berkeley. Watanabe, who had been Japan's high-bar champion, had recently opened his own gym.

Back in northern California, Rip checked out the new gym, the American Gymnastics Center. After five nights of watching Watanabe and his few students through a window, Rip went inside, introduced himself, and observed the workout. On the mats were about a dozen college-age men and one girl several years older than Coral.

The next night Rip brought Coral and Tracee to observe with him. Both girls were amazed; they had never seen training like Watanabe's, nor had they ever encountered a coach who maintained total control by saying almost nothing and never raising his voice.

All the Talaveras switched to Mas Watanabe. Nancy took a weekly gymnastics class for adults and began studying to become a certified gymnastics judge. Rip watched his daughters train for four hours every evening.

In the beginning Rip was not so sure about Watanabe. He spoke so little. Every move was learned by a slow progression from the basics to the more difficult variations. Rip recalled:

"At first I didn't realize how great he was. At times I thought he was holding the girls back, going over basics too often. Then, suddenly, they'd put the moves together *perfectly*. He gave them correct foundations. And the foundation was stronger for Tracee because she was younger and smaller. Earlier coaches had paid more attention to Coral because she was so much better. But she had developed some bad habits from incorrect basics and uneven flexibility. Tracee had the advantage of having been neglected."

Like his daughters, Rip got hooked. His father, Big Rip, brags, "My son was the most devoted student Watanabe ever had. He never missed a workout!"

"Everybody thought I went to watch my daughters," Rip comments. "No way! I went to watch a genius, a master technician. He made gymnastics clean, elegant. I'm a mathematician, a mental gymnast, so naturally I'm drawn to a man who understands the physics behind the moves. He knows *exactly* what he's doing. And because his students mastered the skills so well, they didn't get hurt in his gym. Coral was the star of his team."

Coral explains, "Mr. Watanabe never let you try a move until you felt totally confident. That makes your mind stronger. In competitions we performed better than kids from other clubs because everything we did was with total security."

Before long, Watanabe told Rip that although Coral was his best female gymnast, it was her sister who was championship material. In 1979 Mas Watanabe said, "When the Talaveras came to me, Tracee was only eight or nine. Right away you could see her potential. She's so light and strong for her body size. This makes her agile, coordinated. It is easy for her to learn moves. Plus, she and Coral worked very, very hard.

"Tracee couldn't stand still for a second. In workouts she used to repeat skills twice as many times as Coral did. She had a big advantage in having a sister who was, at that time, a much better gymnast. At home and in the gym Tracee trained with an older, more advanced gymnast. It's important for developing gymnasts to be around better gymnasts."

On the American Gymnastics Center team, Coral competed in Class I and Tracee in Class II. Rip observed every workout and Nancy went to every meet. The only time Coral, Tracee, and Rip missed classes was one month of 1976 when the family took their summer vacation—camping and training in Eugene, Oregon. That summer Coral became a close friend of Leslie Pyfer.

The following year the American Gymnastics Center and the men's gymnastic team at Berkeley thrived under the coaching of Mas Watanabe. His reputation grew. In the spring of 1977 he was appointed Director of Youth Development for the United States Gymnastics Federation, the governing body of the sport. The job was in Tucson, Arizona!

The Talaveras were heartbroken. Where would Coral and Tracee train? The family now faced a big decision. Would the girls quit the sport or would they train somewhere else? It would be a financial burden for the girls to live away from home, but the Talavera family could make it—if that's what the girls really wanted to do.

Coral and Tracee insisted on continuing. They wanted to go to the National Academy of Artistic Gymnastics, in Eugene, Oregon, where they could train with champions like Karen Kelsall, the Canadian Olympian, and the American Elite gymnasts Leslie Pyfer, Amy Machamer, and Jayne Weinstein. It would mean working out seven hours a day, but that was no problem for the supercharged Talavera sisters.

Nancy and Rip decided to give the Oregon move

American Gymnastics Center, Classes I and II, 1976.
The first gymnast is Tracee and the fifth Coral.

a one-month trial during their summer vacation. By the end of that month, the decision was final. Nancy and Rip respected the Academy and its coaches. They had watched their daughters there for parts of three summers. Rip's mind was made up quickly. "What really convinced us to send our girls there was Linda," he said. "No other club in the west has a great woman coach."

Linda, a three-time Olympian (1964, '68, '72), coaches floor and beam; she has a master's degree in dance. Coral loved to dance on the floor and on the beam. Hyperactive Tracee desperately needed help in the dance parts of her floorwork and beamwork.

Tracee and Coral remained in Oregon— remained to train many more hours a day than they attended school. The family had decided that this was the best alternative. But Nancy and Rip had told their daughters, "Whenever you're ready to come home, just give us a call and we'll pick you up at the airport."

Living and training away from home is very expensive—thousands of dollars a year for each girl. Nancy took a job as a clerk-typist in a San Francisco school and spends over two hours a day commuting. Every semester Rip requests more teaching hours. They never go out to dinner or to the movies. Nancy explained, "Gymnastics is our only luxury. For recreation we go running out our front door. It's free."

People often wonder how it is for young children who live away from their parents, but no one seems to ask how it is for the parents. Rip reported:

"It's harder on Nancy than on me. She lives for those weekly phone calls. It's a mental strain for a family to be separated. And it's painful to see your kids do something so dangerous. We always tell Tracee, 'You have one body, only one body without replaceable parts. We want you to keep all your parts intact. We don't want you ruining your knees, ankles or back like so many gymnasts have.' "

After the girls left, I didn't know what to do with my free time. A few days later I bought an eight-week-old pit bull terrier and named her Pitts. For years I had admired the tenacity and courage of pit bull terriers. With the kids away, I could give the puppy the time and attention it needed and deserved. The breeders told us that Pitts had excellent qualities and would make a great show dog. No way! We already have enough competitors in this family."

OREGON

In Eugene, Coral and Tracee shared a room in the dorm, a comfortable home about a half mile from the Academy gym. Dick's mother, Gladys Mulvihill, ran the house, did the shopping, cooking, cleaning, and taxiing.

At first glance the house seemed like an ordinary dorm for teenage girls. But there were a few clues to the contrary. On a living-room table sat the Bible, *Seventeen,* and *International Gymnast.* In the bathroom was a doctor's scale. Taped to the refrigerator were long lists of foods and their caloric content. Along the hallways hung photos of teenagers who had lived there—Nancy Theis, Carrie Englehart, Patti Rope, Karen Kelsall, all of whom were Olympic gymnasts.

Sharing the room next to the Talavera sisters' were Amy Machamer and Karen Kelsall, seasoned international competitors a year older than Coral. Tracee, who had arrived at the dorm just before her eleventh birthday, was the youngest.

In the mornings the gymnasts rose early, ate a light breakfast, then rode off to school on the ten-speed bikes that lined the carport. Coral went to Roosevelt Junior High and Tracee to Adams Elementary. At noon they left school and pedaled back to the dorm for a fast lunch and change. At one o'clock they were dropped off at the gym to earn the academic credits the Eugene schools gave them in P.E., music, and social studies for their training at the Academy. Seven hours later Mrs. Mulvihill would pick up the weary gymnasts and drive them back to the dorm for a hot supper. In the evenings they watched TV, did gymnastics on a bongo board, and disco danced with two experts, Amy and Karen.

That year, 1977—78, Coral and Tracee worked out with the Class I gymnasts. At Christmastime they went home to California for a visit with their parents and the new addition to the family—Pitts.

Back in Oregon, in January Coral injured a tendon in her leg and had to take it easy during workouts. In February Tracee competed in her first international meet. The next morning the Eugene paper had three photos captioned, *"The crowd pleasers: Junichi Shimizu, second in the all-around; Tracy Talavera, second in the girls' all-around; and Olympian Kurt Thomas, men's champ."* After that, the Eugene paper learned to spell Tracee with two es.

Coral nursed her injury and kept up with her daily workouts, but soon she began to ask herself how long she could continue training with the pain. She questioned her belief that "If I work hard enough, get this and get that, I can be in the Olympics."

At the beginning of April, after a particularly hard workout Coral called her parents . . . not to say April Fools. Coral wanted to go home. The next morning her parents met her at the San Francisco airport.

ALONE

Now Tracee was six hundred miles away from Coral; they had always lived together and trained together. Did Tracee miss her family?

"It could be a lot worse than it is," she said. "I have friends here; we all have gymnastics in common—it's the most important thing to all of us. The school isn't too bad, but I'd rather not go to school at all . . . just spend all day in the gym. The only school I liked was kindergarten; we had rats in cages and they had babies!

"I don't think I'm different from a normal kid— just my schedule is different. But what do other kids do after school?"

Wasn't Tracee lonesome without her sister?

"It made me a little sad when Coral left. She influenced me more than anybody else in gymnastics. She got me into the sport. She always used to say, 'Try harder, and no matter what, don't ever quit.' Then, she quit. I realize that she didn't want to be here anymore, but still . . . I guess it doesn't bother me anymore."

Did Tracee ever feel like quitting?

"Never! Sometimes I hate a trick but I never feel tempted to quit the sport. There's just some drive in me that has to work hard at gymnastics. I really want to do it . . . more than anything. I've always been this way—and even more like this since I came to the Academy. I like the training here. There are other kids at the gym who are better than you, so you try to get better than them. When you do, you try to stay better. So, everybody works hard."

After Coral left, Tracee began to prepare for the Emerald Cup, a national meet hosted by the Academy every spring. The hard training brought results. The Eugene paper headlined: ELEVEN-YEAR-OLD BEATS U.S. CHAMP, OLYMPIAN. The article quoted Dick's reaction: "I never expected that. Tracee just walked away with it." But Linda responded, "I'm not surprised."

Tracee continued winning. She won the Western Regional Junior Championship, in which she did a new dismount off the uneven bars. It's a variation of the *Comaneci*, the dismount that Nadia introduced at the 1976 Olympics. But Tracee does the dismount with an extra twist. Some call it the *Talavera*.

Linda predicted that Tracee would win the national junior championship in June. Nancy and her mother, Stella, went to Houston to watch Tracee go for the national title. Although juniors officially were girls aged twelve to fourteen, elven-year-old Tracee was allowed to compete. At 63 pounds, 4'4" Tracee became the youngest American junior champion. Several years before, Nadia Comaneci had won the Romanian Junior National Championship on her eleventh birthday.

After the meet, the three generations—Tracee, Nancy, and Stella—and a plaque shaped like Texas boarded a plane for San Francisco. Back at home in Walnut Creek, Tracee spent a few weeks swimming and bike riding with Coral. Before she returned to Oregon in July, the Talavera family had a conference. Nancy and Rip explained that they might not be able to continue paying for Tracee's gymnastics training. After Proposition 13, the California law that lowered state taxes, many people who worked for the state lost their jobs. Both Nancy and Rip had been told that they might not have jobs in September. Tracee understood that unless both her parents were working, they could not afford the five-to-ten-thousand dollars it cost for a year of training and competing.

When Tracee went back for summer training, her parents explained the situation to coaches Linda and Dick. All summer Tracee worked out without knowing whether she would stay or go home in September. In July, Joy and Big Rip took a vacation to Eugene to visit their younger granddaughter. In August, Nancy, Rip, Coral, and Pitts drove up so that they too could visit Tracee and watch her work out.

At the end of the summer the Talaveras and the Mulvihills talked. By Labor Day Nancy and Rip had learned that their jobs were not in jeopardy, so they could continue paying for Tracee.

Dick and Linda moved Tracee, Karen, and Amy into their home; there, they could monitor their activities and their food intake. The Mulvihill household included Linda and Dick's year-old daughter, Donijo. Also living in the house were Linda's Siamese cats, Natasha and Larissa, and Dick's

Doberman pinscher, Brandy. This year Tracee would train with the Elite group. Every day she would work out with Leslie, Amy, Jayne, and Karen.

After school and workout the whole household eats dinner together; Linda does the cooking. Then everyone helps clean the kitchen, puts away leftovers, and retires to the living room, where there is a huge color TV. Usually Linda and Tracee play with Donijo, who has no interest in TV or going to bed. Exhausted gymnasts lie on the couch or on big pillows on the floor. During commercials people talk. Occasionally Brandy gets excited and Dick tries to calm her down.

Tracee comments, "Gee, too bad Brandy's not smart like Pitts. Brandy tears everything up. She even wants to tear up the neighbors."

Dick sips on his beer and responds, "Oh, that Pitts couldn't find her way out of a paper bag—if you could find one that she wouldn't tear up. When Brandy snaps she's just playing. It's the breed."

Tracee barks, "Pitts knows how to play *right!*"

WARM-UP

Every day Dick and Linda drive to the Academy at 148 West Twelfth Street in downtown Eugene. Out of the car hop Amy, Karen, and Tracee, each carrying a gym bag. Tracee slings hers over a shoulder, over the rainbow suspenders holding up her jeans below a bright yellow shirt featuring John Travolta and Olivia Newton-John. Tracee and Amy crack gum on their way past the bike rack to the gym door.

Once inside the fluorescent-lit gym, the girls go directly to the locker room to prepare for their workout. Dick, heading for the office, greets Leslie Pyfer as she passes him on her way to the locker room.

Tracee comes out of the locker room to take a drink from the water cooler. She is wearing warm-up pants and a warm-up jacket—they're tighter than sweatpants and sweatshirt, so the lines of the body show but the muscles stay warm.

Next to arrive are Jayne Weinstein and her mother, Peggy. Peggy joins Dick in the office while Jayne goes to the locker room to change. Finally, all the girls meet out on the mats.

Tracee shoves her lips out with her tongue and looks down at her clasped hands. She begins twisting them, rotating both wrists, stretching the palms and the fingers. Next, she sits down on the floor near Leslie, extends her body forward, and puts her nose between her shins. Both girls rest there, breathing deeply as their torsos flatten onto straight knees. This position, called the *pike* or *piking* (*jackknife* in diving), is used in all four events of women's gymnastics—floor, beam, bars, and vault.

Without rising, Tracee and Leslie bend their ankles until their toes point to the ceiling. They hold their chests against their knees, with their heads on their shins. Then they sit up, shake their shoulders, and move one leg 180° to the side, the straddle position. Sitting in this split, they slowly bend from side to side, touching shoulder to kneecap. Then they lower the right shoulder inside the right knee and rest on the mat with the right arm extended forward. The left arm reaches over the head to grab the right heel.

Opposite Tracee sits Karen, stretching in this straddle split. Tracee asks her, "What did you do with your fan mail?"

Karen sighs, looking up from the mat to reply, "Well, my mother says every letter has to be answered. But I don't have enough time, so she helps me answer them."

Tracee sits up, puts her hands on her waist, and inquires, "What do they write you?"

"Mostly they ask what color leotards they should buy!"

Along with Jayne and Leslie, Tracee bends to the left, moans, and looks to Karen, who continues, "So,

Tracee pikes down from a
handstand during her floor routine.

Tracee practices arch-ups.
Jodi Lee Kwai looks on.

we tell them to get whatever color they like, whatever they think looks good and fits."

Tracee brings her legs together, leans back onto her hands, slowly slides them backward, and gasps as she says, "Well, I don't think I can answer the two letters I got."

"Why not?" pipe up Jayne and Amy.

Tracee tilts her head and replies, " 'Cause I don't know where I put the letters!" They all giggle, and Tracee slides back farther, stretches out her shoulders, and protests, "But I didn't *mean* to misplace them."

They laugh harder and lean back to loosen their shoulders. Tracee eases her hands slightly to the sides and lies back. Then she bends her arms and legs and pushes her body up into a backbend, in gymnastics called a *bridge.* She straightens her elbows and knees, takes a deep breath, and inches her feet closer to her fingertips. She wiggles her arched body, lightly twisting herself in this stretch for the upper back. Tracee holds her bridge longer than her teammates do. The tightest part of her body is her upper back; when it becomes more supple she will look more graceful, more elegant.

From her high arch Tracee kicks up one leg and then the other, lifting herself into a handstand. She holds this position tightly; her body precisely erect, stretching toward the ceiling. She needs to be as stable in a handstand as normal people are in a foot stand.

Gradually she arches over until one foot and then the other touches the mat, then slowly brings herself up to stand on her feet. She reaches for the ceiling and then back to touch the mat and gently shifts her body through a handstand and over backward to stand on her feet, called a *back walkover*. From here she does a forward walkover—forward onto her hands and over to stand. Then, over backward in another back walkover. Tracee eases through a series of smooth walkovers, exercising control of her back.

After about a dozen walkovers Tracee holds herself in the handstand position for a couple of minutes. Handstands must be aligned perfectly—each of the twenty-six vertebrae directly in line with the one below. Handstands, like foot stands, are maintained by a learned combination of body tension and relaxation; the body responds to gravity through the hands or the feet.

From the endless handstand Tracee suddenly jerks her feet down to land with her toes next to where her wrists were. This, the snapdown, is a basic gymnastic skill and requires great strength in the abdomen.

Slowly Tracee leans forward, transferring all her weight onto her hands. Gradually she lifts her legs until they point straight overhead. From here she pivots, turning her upside-down body by stepping from hand to hand. Above, her arrow-straight body remains still, her toes extended upward. Like a ballet dancer she pirouettes around and around. Later in the workout she will do these pirouettes on the balance beam and still later on the upper bar.

Tracee has had a lot of practice walking in a handstand. For years she and Coral held contests at the two-story home of their Talavera grandparents. They would compete to see who could go up and down the stairs more times without falling off her hands. Usually Coral won.

As Tracee steps from hand to hand, the muscles and joints shift smoothly. The muscles of her back tense and relax rhythmically. After her teammates have come out of their handstands, she snaps down onto her legs. Standing, she exhales through her mouth and swings her head around to loosen her neck. Then she shifts her weight onto one leg and rotates the other ankle, keeping her toes on the mat. Her bones crack.

Amy notes, "Gee, Tracee, your ankles sound like cereal. Snap, crackle, pop! . . . Just be glad you don't have weak ankles like mine!" Amy grits her teeth and shakes one of her feet, almost kicking a coach who has come, coffee mug in hand, to tape Amy's ankles. She hands him a roll of white tape. He takes one foot onto his lap and carefully wraps tape around the foot and ankle.

Both of Amy's feet are securely taped before every workout and meet. This is not unusual for an advanced gymnast; when Linda Mulvihill was competing, she had her ankles taped every day for two years. Occasionally someone else in the Elite group has a sore ankle, knee, or wrist that requires taping for support.

TUMBLING

Before tumbling, Tracee gulps more water while her teammates jog down the mats toward the floor-exercise area. She stares down the tumbling mats, swallows, and steps into a fast front walkover, another, another, and another, all the way there. Near her teammates she stops, and spills her energy by swinging her arms across her chest and then back to clap behind her back.

Tracee jumps, too; she enjoys jumping anywhere and everywhere—on beds and on the spring floor at the gym. The floor contains, between layers of plywood, six thousand small springs which make for higher tumbling and cushioned landings. Over the whole forty-by-forty-foot surface lies a thick, unbroken blue carpet.

Dick stands near the middle of the carpet, hands on hips. He watches these Elite gymnasts until they all look at him. Then he says, "Back walkovers!"

Leslie leads off with a series of walkovers along the diagonal; the end of one begins the next. After she does several, Amy begins, then Karen, then Jayne, and last Tracee. Tracee does four walkovers rapidly. The fifth she does in the air, an aerial walkover, done without putting the hands down. From the take-off, she tosses herself into the air, throws her torso forward, kicks up her split legs, and arches over to land on one foot and then step onto the other.

Back in the corner, Tracee joins the others who lean against the wall. She clasps her hands together and twists her wrists around.

Leslie looks to Dick for instruction. He says, again, "Back walkovers." She turns to face the corner, points one leg at the ceiling, and stretches backward, arching until her palms touch the carpet. She swings the raised leg over her head, her torso rotating until she steps down. Immediately she steps back on the other leg, raising it high again and beginning to arch into her next back walkover.

Like a ballet corps, the girls smoothly, slowly follow one another across the fifty-six-foot diagonal. Hands and feet step down on the diagonal, hips always squared to the direction. This direction and form must be perfected. Without excellent alignment, a series of walkovers on the balance beam could be disastrous.

When Leslie looks up, Dick lifts his palms and tilts the top of his body sideways. She nods and turns sideways to begin cartwheels. She steps to the side and leans over to step down on one hand as her straddled legs swing up over her head. The other hand touches down, the first leg touches down, and she comes up to step on the other foot and move directly into the next cartwheel. The cartwheels get smoother and faster, the movement steadier. Behind her comes a line of gymnasts cartwheeling like precision machinery.

Near the end a small voice cries, "Feet, feet!"

Aligned to do a back walkover.

Immediately Tracee points her toes. From the end corner she looks up and waves to Linda, who has slipped in to watch the tumbling. Linda shakes her head and points one leg directly at Tracee, who points hers back.

Leslie leads off with a row of cartwheels on the other side. They all follow across, smoothly, quickly. At the end Linda calls out, "Form, form! That's a tenth for feet, Tracee." She means that if Tracee used that form in competition, the judges might deduct a tenth of a point from her score. Since Tracee joined the Elite group long after the others, she needs to polish some details that the others have mastered.

Dick struts over to the gymnasts and orders, "Roundoff, flip-flops . . . fast! Tracee first!"

Tracee strides to the front and does a huge skip called a *hurdle*. Out of the hurdle she does a round-off, which begins like a cartwheel. But, before the second hand touches down, she twists her body around to face the direction in which she's moving. With her legs together, she snaps down, yanking her legs down to hit the carpet near where her hands were.

Landing the roundoff, Tracee sinks down, bending her ankles, knees, and hips as she prepares to spring backward. Her arms swing down and then up to the front and back as she springs backward into the air, arching over to land on her hands and continuing over to spring onto her feet. This move, the back handspring, usually called a *flip-flop,* often follows the roundoff. It sets up the gymnast for big backward-tumbling tricks.

Out of the flip-flop Tracee does another flip-flop and another—all the way to the corner. The power to go backward comes from the hurdle into a fast roundoff and quick snapdown.

Because of the way the human body is constructed, some ways of moving are easier than others. For instance, people run faster going forward than backward. But, people tumble higher going backward than forwards. Also, backward tumbling is usually safer than forward tumbling; going backward, you can see your position in relation to the landing surface before touching down. Tumbling forward is often "blind"—the gymnast cannot see the landing surface before touching it.

"Now, Tracee," Dick says, "that form wasn't bad, but you didn't have speed. And you need more arch in the upper back in the first half of your flip-flops. Let's go, everybody. *Faster!*"

They go, and he comments, "Leslie, looking good. Amy, too slow. Jayne, too high—it's slowing you down. Tighter body, Karen. Tracee, more arch in your upper back. Okay, girls, back again. Faster! Faster! Faster! Two more times across . . . everybody faster, and when we get back to this corner, put a back on after the second flip-flop. Go! Faster! Hurry up!"

By *back* Dick means a backward somersault, a complete backward rotation of the body over itself in the air.

In the corner, they breathe hard, all except Tracee. She hops lightly, awaiting the next round.

Dick walks to the opposite corner and shouts, "Roundoff, flip-flop, flip-flop, back! And you need speed for the back. Here's where I want the back!" He taps his toe on a place near the end of the mat.

Leslie nods and begins to run, hurdles into a swift roundoff and into her flip-flops. In her second one Dick yells, "Faster, Leslie!" Her neck muscles tighten and she spins backward, punching up off the carpet and into a back somersault by lifting directly up, tucking her body in tight, and grasping her shins. Beside her, Dick reaches up with one hand, ready to reorient her body if it looks like she might land dangerously. But Leslie completes the somersault without any assistance. On the way down she opens the tuck and reaches for the floor with her feet. She lands bending her ankles, knees, and hips, then lifts her arms into a tall standing pose.

Dick comments, "Not bad, not bad. Okay, Amy!"

Amy swings her arms down behind her, then skips into her hurdle, roundoff, and backward into her first flip-flop. Dick hollers, "Faster, faster, faster!" Amy speeds up. Her back somersault is not as high as the one Leslie did. She lands on her knees, shakes her head, and gets up laughing.

Dick nods at Karen. She hurdles into a roundoff, flip-flop, flip-flop, as Dick yells, "Faster!" He hollers the same word at Jayne and at Tracee.

Dick walks over to the five gymnasts, spreads his legs, folds his arms across his chest, and whispers, "Faster." After they nod seriously, Dick turns around, walks away, winks at Linda, and swivels around from the center of the floor. He clenches his hands into fists, runs rapidly in place, then lets his tongue and arms dangle. When he hears the gymnasts laugh he growls, "Got it?"

Everyone nods, so he waves Leslie on. She

races, tumbling even faster than before. Dick shouts, "All right!" and Linda claps.

Amy hops into her hurdle. Dick runs next to her, challenging, "Faster, faster!" during her flip-flops. Then he hollers, "Punch hard, Amy!" She flies six feet high off the carpet, over Dick's head. He cheers, "Right on, Amy! Now, c'mon, Jaynie . . . fast! . . . Much better, Jaynie. . . . Let's go, Karen."

Karen takes her hands from her ribs and tosses herself into the roundoff and flip-flops as Dick shouts, "Quicker, quicker!" She punches into a high somersault and smiles at Dick on the landing. He leans forward, bows at her, and turns to Linda to say, "Did you see that? High as the one Amy hit!"

Linda cups her hands around her mouth and calls out, "Every somie like that one, Karen . . . especially on beam!"

Karen tilts her head back, pretending to watch someone punch a somersault that high off the balance beam, a somie that begins almost four feet off the ground.

Linda suggests, "Hey, Tracee, perfect form this time!"

Tracee focuses down, tightens her hands into fists, then looks up for Dick's go-ahead. When he gives it, she hurdles into the roundoff, springs backward into her flip-flops, then punches into a back.

Dick walks to her, puts his arm around her shoulder, and escorts her back to where she began, saying softly, "Form was perfect, but what happened to the Talavera speed? This time *fast,* okay?" He bares his teeth like a tiger.

Tracee wets her lips and leads into a fast hurdle,

roundoff, and flip-flops. She punches into a high, high back, lands perfectly, and exhales as she waits for corrections. Dick bends over until his head is level with hers, and says, "See, you can get real high . . . you had enough for a double back then. Let's start working doubles, everybody. First, take off your warm-ups. Your muscles should be warm by now."

The gymnasts peel off their jackets and pants; underneath, each wears a colored, long-sleeve leotard. Leslie wears lime, Amy pink, Jayne gray, Karen purple, and Tracee blue.

Looking at the five in leotards, Tracee clearly is shorter, lighter, and younger than the others. Yet, in tumbling she may have the most experience. When Tracee was seven she could do series of whipbacks—backward somersaults in the layout position, with the body straight. Also at seven, the second-grader taught tumbling.

Her father says, "I used to ride my bicycle past the schoolyard at lunchtime. Tracee would have twenty or thirty kids lined up, doing handstands, cartwheels, basic tumbling. She would holler at them and they loved it! Plus, they were older and bigger than she was and they were from the special class—all deaf or blind."

Tracee remembers those days: "It was *fun!* The blind kids could hear fine, so I just yelled at them. The deaf kids made signals with their hands, so I learned how to do some of the easy signs. One deaf boy was really good; he could hold a handstand forever. And one blind girl was so smart. She used to steal my lunch and eat it up when I wasn't looking!"

Now, from the office at the other end of the gym,

comes the cry: "Dick Mulvihill, long distance!" He jogs to the office.

Linda helps the gymnasts drag a crash mat, six inches deep, onto the open corner of the floor area. Crash mats are not allowed in competitions but they are used in practice to prevent injuries or at least to reduce their severity and to cushion the gymnasts through their many, many landings per day.

A young Japanese man, Hideo "Mizo" Mizoguchi, comes to help carry the crash mat. Mizo directs gynmastics training for boys at the Academy and serves as a technical consultant for bars, vaulting, and tumbling. In 1979 Mizo received a master's degree for researching flip-flop technique.

The gymnasts go to the corner away from the crash mat. Mizo instructs the five gymnasts, "Double backs. But first take one run with a single onto the crash mat. Roundoff, flip-flop, flip-flop back. And once with a single, so you get the feel of these extra six inches on the landing."

Mizo stands at the end, with one foot on the carpet and the other on the crash mat, his hands ready to spot. Every gymnast does the single easily, without a spot or a word from Mizo.

After they have returned to the back corner, Mizo orders, "This time faster . . . and punch off right here—high into a double back. Okay, Leslie, double!"

Leslie nods and races toward him, into her round-off and flip-flops, as Mizo bobs his head in time with her springs off the carpet. When she punches into a good double back somersault, he reaches out to spot her but she doesn't need to be touched. She spins

Graceful Amy leads off. Leaning against the wall are Jayne, Leslie and Tracee.

around twice and kicks out her legs to land on her feet, then falls over and rolls backward onto her hands and knees. In gymnastics it is important to know how to fall without getting hurt. Many Hollywood stuntpersons are former gymnasts.

Amy comes toward Mizo. He hollers, "Faster, faster! Go for it, Amy! Set it up! Not enough. Layout a single, Amy!" Mizo orders her to do a single somersault because she does not have the speed and power to get around twice. He tells her to do it in layout—with a straight body—which is much more difficult than piked or tucked.

Amy flies through the air, rotating her extended 5 ' 6" body all the way around. She is very tall for a competitive gymnast, which makes it harder for her to get her body around itself. However, when she does things well she looks more elegant than any of her teammates.

Amy peers over at Mizo for his reaction. He frowns and runs furiously in place, then waves on the next gymnast.

Jayne tightens her fists and leans forward to break into a fast hurdle and roundoff. During her flip-flops Mizo yells, "Quickly, quickly!" Jayne punches into her double back, flying through the air over the crash pad with her eyes opened wide. Mizo reaches out to spot her lightly on the back, to spin her tucked body around just a bit more. (Mizo spent years training and competing in Japan; there, his coaches spotted his 127-pound body through thousands of double backs.) Smiling, he comments, "Not too bad, Jaynie. Now, put some height into it. Up there, break one of our lights, okay?"

Now he waves at Karen to begin. She rubs her

ribs and races into the hurdle. In her second flip-flop Mizo hollers, "No! *Stop!*" Karen halts and walks back to begin again, while Mizo advises her, "You'll never make a double that slow. Accelerate. Be more aggressive in your flip-flops!"

Karen shuffles, closes her eyes and holds her sides while inhaling deeply. Slowly she exhales and opens her eyes part way. She streaks, punching into a good double, and lands almost erect. Her feet touch the carpet but she falls forward onto her hands.

In the corner, Tracee prepares. She sets her jaw, raises her shoulders, and starts to lean forward into her hurdle. When Mizo shrieks, *"Fast!"* Tracee speeds up, punching into a high double back. Mizo hollers, "Stick it! Stick it!"

Sticking it means ending a trick by landing securely, without wavering or taking any steps. Judges make deductions for any trick that a gymnast does not stick.

Tracee sinks her landing into her feet and then crashes forward onto her knees. She gets up, her head and chest slumped. Mizo puts his arm around her and asks, "Didn't you hear me say stick it? Another ten tries and you'll have it Tracee! . . . Okay, Leslie, you ready? This time you're gonna stick it?"

Leslie nods, then races toward him. She punches high. He steps back from the crash mat and hollers, "Stick it, Leslie, stick it!" She does—almost . . . and then falls backward. Mizo knows she came close. He suggests, "Next time, think *height*. Don't work so hard on your rotation. Think height. More height will give you more time in the air. And, Leslie, your flip-flops are looking better and better."

A door along the back wall opens and a tall man

Tracee in flip flop. Reflected in the mirror is Mizo.

sneaks in and walks over to the piano. He lights a cigarette, folds his arms across his chest, and watches the gymnasts through wire-rimmed glasses. His head bobs with each tumble; he smiles when he sees good tumbling. After a second smoke he wheels in a green bicycle, parks it behind the upright piano, sits down on the bench, and begins playing classical music. He is Art Maddox, the Academy pianist.

Mizo rubs his hands together and inquires loudly, "Who will be the first to stick a double back today? Which one of you five girls? I know all of you can do it."

Leslie sticks one. Mizo leaps into the air and yells, "Hurray!" Linda claps loudly, and the pianist stops playing to look up and see what's happening. Mizo cries out, "Don't we get a smile after that performance? How about a smile, Leslie?" She grins slightly. Mizo shakes a finger at her. "You should be proud of that trick, Leslie! It was beautiful. Now stick it that way every time in every meet."

Next, Amy tries one. She looks unhappy when Mizo screams at her for speed. After she splashes at the end, she begs, "Can I be excused from this now, Mizo? My ankles hurt bad."

He replies, "Yes, but go over to the vaulting runway and practice this doing singles. Just work for speed, Amy. You have to get faster. Push for speed." Amy struts off, disco dancing her way to the vaulting runway against the long wall.

Karen comes to Mizo and says, "My bad knee hurts. I think I ought to rest it."

Mizo responds, "Sure, go over with Amy and work singles for speed."

Like all people, gymnasts have some stronger

and some weaker parts of their bodies. Great coaches know how much to work a gymnast who is coming off an injury. Pain is one of the most important guidelines.

Tracee, Leslie, and Jayne keep working the double backs. Only Leslie sticks them consistently, but Jayne and Tracee usually come close. Finally Mizo announces, "Okay, last time. Now, all three of you, *stick it*. Then tumbling will be over. And, Leslie, double pike."

Double pike means a double back done in pike position, with the legs straight and the hips flexed. Turning is slower in the piked position than in the tight tuck; it takes much more power to do a piked double than a tucked double.

Leslie sucks in her lips, glares at Mizo, and takes off furiously. Down over Mizo's head she spins a double pike and sticks it, raising her hands and taking a light bow toward applauding Linda and Mizo.

He comments, "Just beautiful, Leslie. I bet you eat rice. You do eat rice, don't you?" When Leslie nods in agreement, Mizo shakes his fist at her and then at the others. "I knew it! I knew it! You should all eat rice. Makes you strong—strong as Japanese gymnasts!" He lifts his fists opposite his face, grunts, does a deep knee bend, and everyone laughs.

Linda calls out, "Hey, Karen, Amy, and Tracee—we'll have rice for dinner tonight, okay?" They all nod vigorously and then shrug at one another.

Jayne leans forward from the corner to begin her hurdle. During her flip-flops Mizo yells, "Quickly, quickly! No, Jaynie—take a single." He reaches in to spot Jayne's back, and waits until she lands to advise,

"Better eat rice tonight, Jaynie. Then you'll do it perfectly tomorrow. . . . Okay, Tracee, last try, so make it *stick!*"

Tracee goes and Mizo screeches, "Faster! Go, Tracee! Set up! Go high!" Tracee punches higher than before, sailing around two somies and stretching out her legs to land, as Mizo shrieks, "Stick it, *stick it! Yes! . . . No!* Oh *no!*"

Tracee lands feet first, then crashes backward. She rolls her eyes and picks herself up, groaning and beginning to smile. She rubs the back of her hips, hobbles off the mat, and announces, "I got buttlash! It's worse than whiplash, *buttlash!*"

FLOOR
EXERCISES

Female gymnasts train to compete on four different apparatuses—floor, balance beam, uneven bars, and vault. On each apparatus the gymnast must do compulsories and optionals. For compulsories, all gymnasts do the same set of moves. After each Olympics, a new set of compulsories begins; by Olympics time, competitors have been working those particular compulsories for four years. For optionals, each gymnast performs moves which highlight her strengths.

Academy gymnasts practice optionals every Monday, Wednesday, and Friday; they train for compulsories on Tuesdays, Thursdays, and Saturdays.

COMPULSORY FLOOR

The compulsory floor exercise is a choreographed floor routine done to music by all gymnasts at each ability level. The routine must be done within sixty to ninety seconds. Every Elite gymnast in the world performs the same compulsories. Only changes of side are allowed. Gymnasts leap, jump, split, and twist better on one side than the other, so they do their compulsory floor moves on their better side. Tracee, who is right-handed, does her gymnastics on her left side. She does the compulsory floor routine reversed from the specified way, its mirror image.

The routine features all the basic floor moves, allowing the judges and the audience to compare *how* the contestants do the same movements. Art Maddox explained the difficulty in the compulsory floor: "It's like the driving test. You don't want it too easy; you have to design it so that most people can do it satisfactorily . . . and that means gymnasts in over fifty countries."

Like all athletes, Tracee has definite strong and weak parts of her performance. Her main weakness when she first went to Oregon was dance on both the floor and the beam. Her former coach, Mas Watanabe, noted, "Unfortunately, my gym couldn't provide the dance training Tracee needed. She has improved since she has gone to Oregon. She still needs to improve more, but she has learned so much from Linda."

Dance has never appealed to Tracee, who finds it: *"Boring!* Coral loves it . . . I guess because she's so good at it. I'd much rather work out on bars."

Often, interest in dance increases with age, when gymnasts become teenagers and mature physically. Art feels that Tracee has developed some interest in dance partly to score higher in competitions. He explains:

"At first, all Tracee wanted to do on floor was

tumble. She was totally trick-oriented—working for more and more and more tricks. Most young kids are like that. Leslie used to care only about tricks. It took years for her to learn to turn into a good performer and smile at the spectators. It was gradual for her, and I think it is with Tracee now.

"Right now Tracee doesn't understand delicate moves. She can be exquisite like a blossoming flower or soft like a baby bird. She is developing much more style; when her personality becomes adolescent, she will bloom on floor. Already she looks so much more graceful than she did a year ago."

The compulsory workout usually begins by going through the routine. All five assume the starting pose; Leslie, Karen, and Jayne on the right, with Amy and Tracee on the left. Art plays and they all begin on the same note, all doing the same moves. Yet, they do not look the same.

Tracee, the smallest, does not seem short. When she rises on her toes and spreads her arms she looks like she has a six-foot wing span. But she does not have the elegance of Amy, the power of Leslie, the smile of Karen, or the delicacy of Jayne. Tracee has the energy.

Linda leans on the piano to watch with Art while he plays. They talk to each other until the routine ends and Linda says, "Karen, take it from that leap across the side. Okay, stop. Do it again, and everybody notice how she draws her legs together. One more time, Karen. All of you, try the leap and pull your feet together that fast. Better!"

Art shuffles his track shoes against the floor, rocks his body, and calls out, "C'mere, Amy. Demonstrate

Linda shows Tracee how to position
herself just before finals for the
National Floor Exercise Championship.

a few body waves. You look so *great* doing them. The rest of you, try them and watch yourself in the mirror. Try to make your body like a snake. Watch Amy and keep trying until the waves feel natural. Karen and Tracee, maybe you can work on them at home with Amy?''

Next to Art's bulk, Amy's slender body moves in waves up from her ankles and knees, through her hips, up her back and neck, and seemingly out the top of her head. Amy smiles and speeds up the waves.

Linda walks onto the mat and says, ''Leslie, do the opening tumbling pass and lead into the next movements. Good! Now, when she does it again, everybody watch how she changes, converts from the fast tumbling into the slow, elongated stretch of the whole body with slowly unfolding arms. Dramatic! See how the stretch gets exaggerated when it comes right after the power tumbling with slowed-down arms? Do it once again, Leslie, and then everybody try it a few times across the diagonal.''

After they do it a few times Art calls out, ''Tracee, on your split leaps your front leg goes higher than your back leg. You could get a deduction for that. Try some rows of leaps across the back and watch the height of your legs in the mirror. . . . Nice! Linda, do you notice anything special in those leaps?''

Linda comments, ''Gee, Tracee, you've improved in just this last week. Your legs are opening earlier and staying open longer. Now, think of getting your split as wide as Amy's. And, Amy, try to do yours as fast as Tracee's. Right now, both of you go across together and watch the mirror. . . . Much, much better!''

Linda asks Tracee and Leslie to run through the compulsory. They run to the starting pose and await the music. Lost in playing, Art doesn't realize they are ready. Leslie calls, "Music!" and Linda cries out, "Art!" but he continues playing until Tracee booms, "Hey, Art! Some *vibes!*"

He tosses his head back, and when it comes forward the music for the compulsory begins. They run through the routine in a little over a minute. When they finish, Linda compliments them and then asks for the last tumbling run several more times.

After the fifth time Leslie frowns and begs, "Can't we work something else?"

"Yeah, this part is *gross!*" adds Tracee, pounding her fists into her hips.

Linda raises her eyebrows at Tracee and Leslie before responding, "Okay, you two, you win. Take it from the back walkover."

They run to another part of the floor and begin leaning backward, ready to reach for the floor on the right note. Linda instructs, "I want this part smooth. Onto the hands and then back onto the feet like you're stepping onto clouds. . . . Better! A few more times. And, Tracee, perfect form on every move. Whoops! Stop right there. Tracee, you've got to follow the music, honey. You're off. If Art is playing he can follow you, but when you compete with a tape cassette you *have* to follow the music."

Art explained that good gymnasts "turn on" while competing. The better their performance, the more likely they are to be out of time with the music. However, a good musician can play notes sooner or later to stay in time with the moves of the gymnast.

Tracee and Julianne in compulsory floor.
Behind them are younger Class II gymnasts.

Good gymnasts often tumble faster and leap longer at meets.

"The tougher the competition, the more flexibly I have to play—especially in the Olympics," Art said. "It's very demanding on me. Other sports done to music—ice skating, synchronized swimming—always use recorded music. I play live so that I can accommodate the timing and rhythms of the gymnasts; if the music is not with the gymnast, she can get a deduction.

"Great performers like Nadia and Olga *turn on* at meets; Leslie, Tracee, and Amy do too! It's easiest for me to play well for the kids from our gym. I know them best, their gymnastic abilities and their personalities. It's easy for me to read their emotional states, to know how turned on they are. And I'm familiar with where they tend to speed up and where they tend to slow down. Dick always says that great music played perfectly raises a floor score two- to four-tenths."

Art looks to Tracee and Leslie before advising them, "Listen, you characters, loosen it up. No more wooden gymnastics. This time loosen up so every movement is *you*. You've got to feel it, feel every move from inside. Feel it and let us see how much you enjoy doing it. *Own* it! Last time, so—perfection! Amy, Karen, and Jayne, you're on after them."

Amy, Jayne, and Karen stand by with Linda to watch. Art begins to play; Tracee and Leslie inhale and swell an inch higher in the opening pose, ready to begin on the right note. Just before it Linda stage-whispers, "Form!"

At the finish, Linda jumps into the air, clapping.

"Oh joy! Joy! Tracee pointed her toes all through the routine. Beautiful, Tracee. You looked so long-legged." Tracee rolls her eyes.

From the other side of the piano comes Dick's strong voice: "And when we get to Hungary, I want you two to watch those Hungarian, Russian, and Romanian gymnasts closely. They're very good at compulsories—especially the Russians, the best in the world."

The week after the U.S. team returned from Hungary, the team musician, Art, and the team coach, Dick, and four of the six competitors—Tracee, Leslie, Amy, and Jayne—showed Linda where the compulsories differed from the way the Americans were doing them.

Tracee demonstrates as she says, "Linda, right here in this turn they looked sideways before they brought their arms up. We never look sideways."

Linda sips her diet soda and replies, "Do it three times our way and then three times their way. Again."

Art rises from the piano bench and does the turn with Tracee. He notes, "See, it went that way with the face, but look at how the torso holds the vertical during the twist until the next note. Their line looked better than ours. Tracee, will you do the part to music a couple times? Thanks. I'll play for you."

He races back, and plays and replays it while Linda kneels in front of Tracee, shifting her torso to various angles while asking Amy, Jayne, and Leslie to comment. Then Linda exclaims, "I got it! Much, much better their way! Maybe we can all put in a bit of that lean and hold it until just before Art hits the next note. Adds elegance. Great! What else did they do that we can incorporate? Say, Art, the movies you and Dick shot in Hungary just arrived—why don't you come over to our house tonight and we can study them together . . . maybe pick up some other details to improve our compulsories.''

OPTIONAL FLOOR

On days when the gymnasts do their optional floor exercises, they take turns working individually with Linda and Art. While one gymnast works with the coaches, the others practice details or rough spots in their routine.

Linda and Art act as if they have been working on floor exercises together forever; actually it has only been since 1963. That year the gymnastics coach at the YMCA in Champaign, Illinois, decided to splurge by hiring someone to compose music for his best gymnast, fourteen-year-old Linda Metheny. He called the music department of the University of Illinois; they referred him to an electronic-music composer, Art Maddox, who accepted the job. Over the next few months Art composed the music for Linda's optional floor routine. She used it at the 1964 Olympics, both at trials and at the games. Later she performed to Maddox's arrangements in the '68 and '72 Olympics. And who was the Y coach who paid for her first composition out of his own pocket? Dick Mulvihill.

Linda continued gymnastics training under coach Mulvihill, became a college gymnast, earned a master's degree in dance, and married her first coach.

Soon after the '72 Olympics, Linda and Dick moved west to found the National Academy of Artistic Gymnastics, "dedicated to excellence in competitive gymnastics." They settled on Eugene, a sports-minded community near mountains and ocean. Art moved to Eugene too. He has played piano and choreographed with Linda since the Academy opened, except for the two years he spent earning a Ph.D., awarded in 1979, for his thesis "Music in Women's Artistic Gymnastics—Floor Exercise."

Art first met the Talavera sisters near the end of his 1978 New Year's visit to Eugene. He recalled, "Instantly I could see that Coral looked great on floor, but Tracee . . . just watching her, I sensed the potential that Dick and Linda had already recognized. She was strong and inexhaustible. What challenged me was trying to find her limits. She could tumble, tumble, tumble, without even breathing hard.

"After watching her closely—her compulsory floorwork, her old optional routine, and her behavior around the gym—we realized what she needed. So there, during the last days of what was supposed to be my vacation, Linda and I worked together to make a new routine for her. We decided to use the tune 'Games People Play.' We tried moves with her, reworked them, tried series of moves, fiddled with them, and finally got together a routine to fit Tracee."

Five weeks later, on February 13, 1978, sixth-grade Tracee used that routine at her first international competition. The Eugene paper reported,

"Her floor exercise was spiced with comical spurts that brought the house down." The story began under three photographs, one of which showed the final pose of Tracee's optional floor routine—standing on one leg, the other crossed over at the knee, leaning over her bent knee with one arm extended overhead and the other bent with the palm open under her smile.

For two years Tracee used the basic floor routine. With mastery of more difficult tumbling tricks, they replace the easier ones. Sometimes the music or number of steps has to be changed slightly. Gradually Linda has helped Tracee polish her moves to smooth out her routine. However, reports Art, "The theme continues to be her energy."

After working with Jayne on floor, Linda and Art talk. Jayne joins her teammates in their contest across the floor. They are seeing who can walk across the mat fastest, on their hands. On each step they scissor their legs. Linda cries, "Form!" and everyone's hips lift, the toes point harder, and the legs split further. Amy's legs go wider than the split—both her feet are lower than her hips.

Art shouts, "Hey, Tracee, your turn!"

She comes off her hands and runs directly to her starting position. Linda walks to her, changes the placement of one foot, tilts her head, and rounds her elbows. Then, smiling, Linda waves at Art to begin the music.

After a few notes Tracee begins. Linda and Art watch approvingly until the end of the second tumbling run, when she jumps into the air and spins a full turn in the air. On her landing the music stops. Tracee wrinkles her nose and looks from one coach to the other. Both hold up two fingers. When Art shouts, "Doubles!" Tracee clucks her tongue and tries. Up into the air she jumps, going for two whole turns, the double. After a few tries she gets around twice.

Tracee walks back to her starting pose and awaits the music. This time she performs faster and Art plays faster. When it's time for the jump, Linda cries out, "Up, honey!" and Tracee flies.

Linda jogs over, puts her arm around the gymnast, and says, "Okay, Tracee. Now let's go through your whole routine without stopping. Double—and remember, perfect form, head up to the ceiling. Communicate with your audience. The judges will appreciate that."

Floor exercises are the only event in which gymnasts can look at the audience. In beam, bars, and vault they must focus on the apparatus. The floor, the "personality event," allows the exceptional gymnast to make herself felt by every spectator, to project the way great ballerinas and actresses do.

Near the end of the run the music suddenly stops. Tracee turns to the piano and frowns. Art advises, "Tracee, you need to go faster at the end. For practice your tumbling looks okay but for competition you need more speed to get higher somies. Go faster!"

Tracee objects, "But I can't go any faster!"

Art scowls, pushes himself up from the piano bench, and strolls over to her, claiming, "Tracee can go as fast as the speed of light!"

She shrugs, and he walks behind her, chuckles at Linda, and begins twisting an invisible key in the center of Tracee's back. Then he exhales loudly and announces, "Now Tracee will go faster than the speed of light."

He returns to the piano, sits down, shoves his glasses back onto the bridge of his nose, lifts his wrists, and begins to play. And Tracee explodes across the mat.

In her last tumbling run Art yells over his music, "All right, Tracee! Think of the extra tenth that will get you! Didn't that feel faster?"

Tracee shrugs and yawns as she walks to the edge of the mat. Art calls out, "Hey, honey, we're not done. We've got a problem down in this corner by me. Tracee, every time you pivot here, your arms look awkward. Let's see you try some arm variations."

Tracee runs to the corner and begins pivoting with exploratory arm moves. Linda, 5'2", joins 4'9" Tracee and 6'3" Art. All three pivot, experimenting with their arms.

Amy steps onto the mat and pivots with them, swirling her arms gracefully. Linda notices Amy and suggests, "Tracee honey, watch Amy and try some of the moves she does. . . . Okay, much better. This time, try raising only the outside arm. Keep the other one down—and watch the arm while you lift it, focus on your hand. . . . Great! Now, do it a few more times so you'll have it. Try the whole phase; Art will play for you."

Tracee scampers back to the opposite corner, ready to tumble across the diagonal and end doing the pivot with the new arm movement. After the fourth time, Art shouts, "Right on, Tracee! Amy, you ready?"

Linda extends Tracee's arms while she
jumps backwards. Notice the lines of Tracee's
arms and the width of her shoulders.

Arms still exploring, Amy asks, "Can we do a new arm move for me too? I love to do arms."

Linda walks to Amy and asks what changes she wants to make. They try out some arm moves together.

BALANCE BEAM

The balance beam is the only apparatus designed for female gymnasts. The floor and the vault are the same for women and men, and the uneven bars are men's parallel bars set at uneven heights. Top gymnasts can do on beam almost everything they do on floor. Staying balanced on the beam requires alignment; the center of gravity must stay over the beam, which is less than four inches wide.

Since many people have seen gymnastics only on television, they are most familiar with beam. Of the four women's events it is the least distorted by TV and the easiest to film. Usually the beam is shown from the side, with the gymnast silhouetted.

Fans love watching beamwork. As with tightrope walking, it is easy to see when a fall is about to occur. And it can be thrilling to see a gymnast struggle to recover, to regain her balance and remain on the beam.

Beam is the clutch event of women's gymnastics. While all competitions are stressful to gymnasts, the balance beam pressure-cooks them. In major meets even the best competitors fall or do not complete beam routines within the time limit, which is one minute and fifteen to thirty-five seconds. Deductions for being under time (too fast) were made on the beam scores of Stella Zakarova at the '79 American Cup and Nadia Comaneci at the '79 World Cup. At the '76 Olympics, Olga Korbut received a deduction for being over time (too slow) on beam.

Falls off the beam are the most obvious effect of stress at meets. At the '76 Olympics, five of the six American gymnasts fell off the balance beam. At the '79 National Sports Festival, in the beam finals every gymnast but one lost her balance—every one but the youngest, twelve-year-old Tracee Talavera, who won the meet, the beam, and the bars.

Not everyone agrees on why top gymnasts who rarely fall off the beam in practice fall off in meets. Coral Talavera, who excelled at beam, believes that falls happen because of loss of concentration. "Being mentally ready for a meet is as important as being physically ready," Coral said. "It's your mind, not your body, which blows tricks, makes you fall. My sister doesn't just put her body into gymnastics; her mind is there too. She doesn't depend on just her body. She thinks about everything she's going to do. Isn't that right, Mom?"

Nancy Talavera, a certified gymnastics judge, agreed. "Most kids aren't mentally strong enough for competition. The other gymnasts don't wipe them out; they wipe themselves out. When I'm judging, I can predict, by the way a girl presents herself to the judges, whether she will make her routine or blow it."

Rip added, "The crucial thing is whether you're trained mentally as well as physically. Most American coaches don't understand that; they're too busy thinking strength and big tricks. The difference with Tracee is that she had two years with Mas Watanabe. He developed her mentally, developed her confidence. He never allowed her to do anything in a meet until she was hitting it one-hundred-percent in the gym. She got used to *always* hitting. Most coaches aren't like that; Coral calls them gophers—they coach by yelling 'Go-fer-it!' "

At meets, fans often cheer gymnasts from their own club, state, or country, or whoever they expect will win. After Tracee won the bars title in '79 at Madison Square Garden, she performed in beam finals with thirteen thousand fans yelling, "Tracee! Tracee! Tracee!"

Most gymnasts claim they block out everything once they approach the balance beam. Didn't Tracee hear them screaming for her! She recalled, "In the back of my mind I could hear them, and it made me feel good, made me relax. But I don't pay attention to the crowd. I just try to do my best."

From only a few feet away from the beam Linda watched Tracee perform. Does Linda think the screaming spectators affected Tracee? "Huge crowds don't faze her. All the way through her routine the arena echoed 'Tracee!' but it didn't throw her off. She got the highest beam score of the meet, the highest of her life then, a 9.6."

Was Tracee nervous before the American Cup competition? Art commented, "Tracee nervous? Ha! All she did was talk up the trip . . . without mentioning gymnastics, Madison Square Garden, or New York City. She wasn't a bit nervous! But she was *very* eager. All she ever talked about was where they were going after the meet—to Disney World in Florida. For two weeks she talked about the rides she would go on."

Gymnasts spend more time practicing beam than any other event. Tracee prepares for her daily two- to two-and-a-half-hour beam workout by "watering" her stomach. At the watercooler she inhales air and water from the arched stream.

She walks to a high beam and mounts it. *Mounting* means getting onto a piece of apparatus; in this case, getting on top of the beam, 120 centimeters (3'11") high. In workouts, gymnasts usually use the simplest mount, which looks like a swimmer getting out of a pool. Tracee puts her hands on the top of the beam, then hops up from the mat and positions herself to stand up on her left foot outside her left hand. She uses this mount about fifty times per workout, always onto the left foot.

Up on the beam, Tracee looks at one end and walks to it. There she pivots, looks to the other end, and goes toward it. After a dozen passes she looks sideways at her reflection in the wall of mirrors parallel to the six high beams. She stands there swelling her torso while lowering her shoulders, rounding her arms, and lifting her head. She does not notice her teammates and their reflections even when they pass between her and the mirror.

Sharply Tracee twists, glares down to the far end of the beam, and points one foot forward. Her toes curl over the edge of the beam, the heel over to the other edge. Slowly Tracee transfers her weight forward, the toes grip the edge and wrap over the side of the beam, the instep crosses the middle, and the heel touches the other edge of the beam. Gradually she

Linda tells Tracee to extend more.

shifts her weight onto the front foot, lifts the back one, and draws it forward to reach the edge of the beam with pointed toes.

On the mat, Linda walks along the ends of the beams. Occasionally she says to Tracee, "Square your hips." Immediately Tracee evens her hips so that if a line were drawn vertically through them it would be perpendicular to the beam. Within an hour she will be somersaulting on this beam. If her alignment is not perfect she could fall and injure herself.

Tracee makes about ten slow passes down the beam. Then she stares into the mirror again. She shakes her body loosely and straightens herself up and down, lifting her torso so that the bottom of her rib cage comes into definition above her stomach muscles.

Next, Tracee puts her hands on her hips, lifts her face, and minces one foot a few inches to the side. Calmly she transfers her weight to that side and draws the other foot in. Then she again moves her foot sideways as she watches herself in the mirror, focusing on her form. She steps from foot to foot all the way along the beam, holding her chest high, her head erect, her focus always on her reflection.

At the end, she turns and minces back to the other end. When Linda whispers, "Tummy," Tracee sucks her middle in farther. Her ribs project and the muscles bulge down her back.

Tracee does one more walking pass with toes pointed to wrap around the edge of the beam as she steps forward. After she pivots, she raises her back leg behind her to hip height, slowly moving it around to the side and then directly forward before lowering it to step forward. The quadriceps at the top of her raised thigh enlarges; it is the largest muscle in the body.

Gymnasts do not speak during beamwork; they focus on alignment, placement, the lines of the body balanced over the beam. The only words spoken are those few of correction or praise from Linda. In order to stay on the beam, the gymnasts must maintain total concentration.

For about an hour the gymnasts do only these slow balancing moves, getting themselves into the feel of the beam, getting away from the floor tumbling. After these basic exercises to perfect their form and steady themselves, they will begin tumbling on beam.

Linda directs the beam practice. As a gymnast she did her best performances on the beam—the only American woman to qualify for an Olympic final. She earned the highest Olympic place an American woman has ever reached, fourth in the balance beam, five one-hundredths of a point out of third place, the Bronze Medal position. The 1972 Olympic guidebook describes Linda Metheny as "the steadiest gymnast America has ever produced." When she was appointed head coach of the 1980 Olympic team, Linda looked forward to the opportunity to coach some Americans to break her fourth-place record and to win America's first Olympic medals for women's gymnastics—perhaps in her best event, the balance beam.

The balance beam itself has changed since the late 1960s, when Linda Metheny and Cathy Rigby were our best gymnasts. Now the beam itself is padded, covered with imitation suede that absorbs perspiration, reduces slippage, and cushions landings. Inside the beam itself, under the top layer of wood rests a layer of foam that allows a bit of spring for take off and more cushioning for landing aerial tricks.

In the 1968 Olympics, beamwork was mainly dance moves, balances, and slow acrobatics. Now, beamwork uses tumbling tricks that were not done even on the floor ten years ago. The "Wide World of Sports" TV documentary on women's gymnastics shows the 1968 Gold Medal beam routine featuring a handstand, and narrates, "Our contrast is in the American Cup, 1979. Tracee Talavera. Watch her acrobatic moves! . . . She's so much more aggressive. She almost attacks her moves!"

Her sister Coral comments, "Tracee has always been really gutsy. She'd fight kids who wanted to fight. I was afraid to fight them, but not Tracee. She's always been that way. That's how she does the beam—aggressively!

"In our San Francisco elementary school, almost all the kids were black. Sometimes they would tease us at recess. I would run away, find a teacher, and hold her hand. The other kids would be yelling at us, 'You white honkies!' Tracee would yell right back at them, 'I am *not!* I'm *brown!*' "

By *Brown* Tracee meant Mexican-American or Chicano. Talavera de la Reina ("Tiara of the Queen") is a town near Madrid, Spain, where Big Rip's father was born. Nancy's mother was born in Mexico.

Rip described Tracee's behavior: "Tracee was always playing tough with the black kids. It was before busing. She would race around like a bee; nobody could ever catch her. She learned to be tough there. Tracee is not afraid of anything or anybody. Our balcony overlooked the schoolyard. Every recess Coral would be holding the hand of a white teacher, but not Tracee! She was out there being rough with the other kids. She was the smallest one, but nobody beat up Tracee! Nobody! She's like me—in fact, she's a carbon copy of me as a kid ... . only, she never gets hurt."

Tracee is the only one on her team who has not been injured while doing gymnastics. Everyone else has broken bones, torn ligaments, pulled muscles, or sprained joints. Tracee has never missed a workout because of injury, and this has enabled Tracee to develop consistently, without backsliding. Dick Mulvihill believes that missing a day sets the gymnast back a week; losing a week sets the gymnast back a month or two.

Why hasn't Tracee been injured? Luck? Linda believes it is due to Tracee's sense of space and body position. She said, "Tracee reminds me of my cats; it isn't that she never falls . . . everybody does. It's that when she does fall, she recovers so quickly, so well. Even when she falls head-first, she rights herself before landing."

Though many people think of beamwork as merely elevated floorwork on a narrow plank, the beam is not flat. The shape of the beam permits the hands and feet to work around its curved edges, to grip the sides, which obviously cannot be done on the floor. Steadiness and balance on the beam can come from pressure applied by strong, articulated toes and fingers.

In the warm-up on beam, Tracee does a series of

walkovers. Her hands reach out for the beam. But, very little of her hand touches the top of the beam. Only her thumbs rest on the surface. Her palms fan out to the sides of the beam and her fingertips press against the sides of the beam. The palms extended to the sides allow Tracee to balance over a wider base, about six inches rather than four.

In forward or backward walkovers Tracee easily sees the beam before placing her hands. However, in rapid tumbling, especially in a series of fast moves, there is little time to correct or change hand placement. Positioning must be perfect. And positioning improves through daily repetition, thousands of times of moving onto and off of the hands.

Learning to be steady on the hands might seem nearly impossible. But think about how you learned to be steady on your feet. Babies spend months learning to stand and to walk. They fall thousands of times before they can walk securely. They work through the frustration by improving slowly. Gymnasts do the same slow learning. Tracee, however, has always been a fast learner of basic motor skills. She walked when she was eight months old.

After Linda feels that the gymnasts have warmed up enough on beam, she sends them for their notebooks. In her notebook each gymnast writes how she did each routine; the books provide a progress report. If a gymnast falls or wobbles during a routine, she has to note it. At the Academy all Class I and Elite gymnasts keep notebooks for beam and for bars.

Notebook in hand, each gymnast gets a drink before beginning her daily beam routines, twenty

compulsories or fifteen optionals. Before mounting the beam, each gymnast puts her notebook near the base of the apparatus.

COMPULSORY BEAM

The compulsory mount for beam requires great control and strength in the upper body—shoulders, arms, and back, where, comparatively, Tracee is strongest. Standing at one end of the beam, she lifts her hands and lowers her palms onto the beam, shoulder-width apart with the ends of her fingers reaching down around the far side of the beam. She stares at herself in the mirror and then looks down at her hands.

Gently she jumps off the mat, lifting her hips higher than her shoulders, and shifts her weight forward. Through her hands dive her pointed toes, and, without touching the beam other than with her hands, she rotates her body around her shoulder joints until her feet are behind her head and her hips are forward, almost as high as her shoulders. At this point Linda steps in, pushes the small of Tracee's back higher, making her line smoother, her back parallel to the floor. Over the next nineteen routines the height of Tracee's hips increases. Each time she begins her mount, Linda is there, suggesting more height.

From this dramatic mount the gymnast lowers her hips to the beam, arches her body, and spreads her arms wide behind her for a second before putting her hands down.

Concentration is essential before placing hands on the beam to begin a routine.

Arms moving forward in the
compulsory beam. See the long
lines of the spine and legs.

*Minutes before mounting the beam
for compulsories, Tracee quietly focuses
on aligning herself on the sidelines.*

Tracee and her teammates rarely fall during compulsory beam practice. When they do, it usually follows a lapse in concentration. The beam demands total attention. And in competitions there are many other things to interest the competitor, in addition to the press of the meet. At the '79 American Cup, commentator Cathy Rigby Mason said when Tracee mounted the beam, "Yesterday everybody expected her to be a little bit wobbly because this is her first international meet . . . and this is the event that takes so much concentration. She pulled off one of the most fantastic routines of the day on this event!"

After each routine Tracee picks up her notebook and, usually, makes another mark under her "Completed Routines" section, so that by the end of beamwork it looks like all right, okay, good, awful. If she wobbles or loses her balance at all, she notes that.

OPTIONAL BEAM

On optional-routine days the beam workout lasts longer than on compulsory-routine days. This means that after the warm-up, the gymnasts spend another hour and a half on their optional routines.

Before mounting the beam Tracee practices her optional tricks. She works them down the seam of the mat because, if she should lose her balance and fall, there is much less chance of injury. Once the tricks are done smoothly along the seam, Tracee works them on a beam without a base; this means that the top surface of the beam is only inches above the mat. Her alignment must be good if she is to stay on the

Linda tells Tracee to point more
as she works her tricks down the seam.

beam. However, if she should fall, the mat is closer than it will be from the high beam.

Tracee has a difficult optional beam routine. She does hard tricks and several series of difficult ones. On beam it is much harder to do a series than to do each trick separately. The landing of a trick serves as the take-off position for the next one. Any misalignment at the end of a trick becomes exaggerated in the next trick and further multiplied in the third one. For this reason, gymnasts do warm-up tumbling series down a line on the mat before working them on a low beam and then onto a high one.

Somehow, Linda always knows when Tracee is about to mount the beam. By the time Tracee has put the springboard into exactly the right place by the center of the beam, Linda is standing near her, waiting to give corrections.

Tracee concentrates, focusing on the beam. Then she takes two steps to the board, lays her hands on the beam, and jumps onto the springboard. As she bounds off the board, she leans her weight onto her left hand and swings her straight legs to the right. The straight body swings past where the right hand had been and continues forward as the right hand comes down again. She shifts her weight to the right as she swings her legs to left and then backward, completing the circle, and then she leans to the left again so that her legs come to rest to the right along the beam.

This unique mount uses a technique developed by men and used on the pommel horse, with its three-foot-long bolster and two high handles for gripping. As on the pommel horse, this move requires great body control, timing, and upper-body

Tracee flip flops on low beam.
Notice how her fingers reach for the
top and sides of the beam.

strength, as well as balance in all directions. Judges may award extra tenths for originality in this mount. Since the mount is the first trick, this one "lets the judges know this gymnast is somebody special," notes judge Nancy Talavera.

Tracee and Linda constantly refine the routine, changing small parts to improve performance or enhance the lines. Linda asks, "What do you think of that foot coming through then, Tracee . . . do you think it might be better held back a split second longer? Take that part over a few times, and hold the leg different amounts of time . . . which one feels best to you?"

Tracee tries, experimenting with holding her leg slightly different amounts of time. As she tries, she watches herself in the mirror. Linda says, "Why not try to hold it until that front arm goes just above your head. It changes the rhythm, jazzes up that part, and gives better continuity into your next move. Let's try."

Linda and Tracee try together, Tracee on beam and Linda below on the mat next to the beam. They compromise on how they like it best. Tracee does it the new way, holding the leg longer. Then she begins several moves that she uses earlier in her routine, to work the leg hold in with a series, integrating it into her routine.

Long before she went to Oregon, Tracee had another great beam coach, Coral Talavera. Coral loved beam; she usually scored higher on beam than on the other three events. She said about beam, "We worked so much on beam, so many hours in our living room, that I didn't fall off . . . it helped Tracee too. For beam you need to block out the rest of the world . . . even in a noisy arena with spotlights you *have* to be alone. You *cannot see* anything but that beam."

Remembering her work on beam in Oregon, Coral added, "Linda has such a good way of putting things together . . . she does the choreography *with* you. Most coaches force kids to do what they want the kids to do. That makes the kids do some moves they hate, so they look lousy. If you don't feel great doing something, you won't do it well.

"Linda understands about the body. One coach we had kept pushing me to do front walkovers across the beam; I always got a high score for it because nobody else could do it. Later we saw some Russians do it. But it hurt my back to do it. When I told Linda about it, she asked me to show it to her once. Then she told me she didn't want me doing it if it hurt me. She doesn't push for tricks that hurt you just to get extra points in a meet."

When Tracee first went to Oregon she liked bars as much as Coral liked beam. Now Tracee likes beam more than she used to. And her beam scores are usually as high as her bars scores. At the '79 American Cup and the '79 National Sports Festival, Tracee won both the bars and the beam.

During her first two years in Oregon, Tracee learned to move smoothly between her difficult tumbling tricks on beam. Slow, graceful moves between speedy tumbling make for a more dramatic performance.

At the end of her routine Tracee dismounts in a way designed to amaze judges and spectators. From one end of the beam she begins a very rapid tumbling pass—four aerial tricks nonstop. She begins with an aerial cartwheel, right into a flip-flop, another flip-flop, then into a 1½ twister off the end of the beam. In the dismount she does a back somersault with 1½ twists around herself before landing.

Tracee sticks her dismount and then sits down on the mat. Is she sitting because she feels wiped out? No. She's sitting to write in her notebook. Before she writes, her chin juts out and rests on her hand. Then she writes quickly, puts the notebook by the base of the beam, and goes to position the springboard.

Tracee backs off two steps and begins staring at the beam. Linda watches. Tracee steps forward to jump off the board and begin her mount that circles the beam.

After a dozen routines Linda comes to Tracee while she's writing in her notebook. Linda leans over to say, "What do we need to work?"

Tracee stops writing, pulls on her middle toes, and asks, "My somie?"

Linda nods. Tracee says, "Just a sec," and runs to get a drink of water. She rushes back to help Linda pull a one-foot-thick crash mat under the beam. They place it right under the center of the beam, as extra protection for working many somies. Tracee hops back onto the beam, up on her left foot. She stands in the middle of the beam and concentrates.

Linda advises, "Throw a few somies. I want to watch to see why they don't look so good today."

Linda goes to the end of the beam and leans her elbows against it. She watches eight or nine somies before commenting, "Tracee, honey, I think you need to slow it down just a bit. Try a few slower. . . .

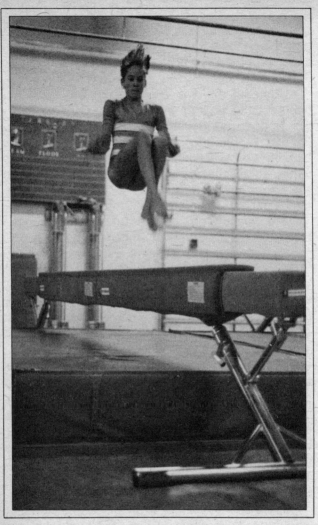

Tracee lands a somie. To reduce the chance of injury, the beam is wrapped with padding and set low over a crash mat.

Yes! Better! A few more. . . . Okay, now from the last one pass right into the slower somie. No, on the finish come out big and tall."

Linda rises to the tips of her toes, throws her arms up, and looks at the ceiling. Tracee nods and then throws a few, ending in the pose Linda demonstrated.

Tracee does steady somies. Watching her on TV in the American Cup competition, Art Maddox noticed, "She stood that somie up *cold*! I never saw any gymnast do a cleaner somie. It was fantastic! And her look reminded me of Comaneci, that fierce determination, that look you so rarely see on anyone, especially a young girl."

One day Dick walks out of the office and stops near Linda, who is watching Tracee mount the beam. Halfway through Tracee's routine, he leans toward Linda and remarks, "Look at that concentration. She's so *determined*. Nothing will get her off that beam. That's what makes her so tough in meets."

When Tracee sticks her dismount, Dick asks, "How many, Tracee? Fourteen? Okay, before your last one get into the belt."

Tracee writes in her notebook and then runs to get the twisting spotting belt, which is a metal circle with belts inside. Tracee drops it on the mat, steps into the center, and pulls it up to her waist. She stuffs a piece of foam between it and her back, then buckles the belt.

Dick walks across the mats to the wall and loosens the cords tied to the wall fixture. The cords slip out so that the other two ends, which have clips, come down from the ceiling pulleys to the sides of the beam that Tracee will mount. She clips each end to her spotting belt and climbs onto the beam.

From the middle of the beam, Tracee loosens the cords attached to her waist so that they hang in big loops from her sides. She focuses on the other end of the beam and doesn't move until Dick asks, "Okay?"

Tracee walks to the far end of the beam, pivots, and focuses on the other end. She tumbles. Aerial cartwheel, flip-flop, flip-flop. As she lands her second flip-flop, Dick yells, "Punch!" and Tracee drives high off the end of the beam into her dismount. Near the top of her flight off the beam, Dick yanks on the cords to lift her higher as she twists.

She sticks her dismount and then looks to him for corrections. He says, "That's how to drive it up there, Tracee! Make like you have room for a triple. Think *up!* A few more times. Remember, it's the last trick the beam judges will see."

Tracee scampers back onto the beam, pulls on the cords so that they dangle from the clips at her waist, and walks to the end. There she adjusts her focus, intensifies her concentration, and charges for the other end of the beam. Dick bites his upper lip, yanks on the cords, and shouts, "Stick it, Tracee! Stick it!"

UNEVEN
PARALLEL BARS

The uneven parallel bars is the only women's event where the body is supported mainly by the hands. In floor, beam, and vault, the weight is usually on the feet. In contrast, four of the six men's events are hand-support events—rings, parallel bars, pommel horse, and horizontal bar, but not floor and vault. Women used to do all the men's events, including the flying rings, which was banned for men in the 1960s because it caused too many serious injuries.

Bars is the newest women's event. Until 1950 women performed on the same parallel bars that men used—pairs of rails at the same height, shoulder-width apart. Uneven bars began by using men's parallel bars with the rails set at different heights.

Uneven parallel bars is now a separate apparatus. The two rails are set at regulation heights of 2.3 meters (7'6") and 1.5 meters (4'11"). The adjustment for different lengths of body and arms is made by moving the lower one within the allowable distance from the higher one between 48 and 68 centimeters (1'7" to 2'3").

Uneven bars used to be made of wooden rails; now, rails are made of fiberglass laminated with a thin wooden veneer. The fiberglass has several advantages over wood: it is stronger and lasts longer, and it has less variation, so sets of rails are more similar in their "give."

Manufacturers have yet to standardize the shape of the rails themselves. The two leading companies make different-shaped rails! One makes the rails pear-shaped, like men's bars, and the other makes the rails round, like men's horizontal bar. Female gymnasts compete on both shapes, on whatever apparatus is provided for competition. However, each of the two shapes requires a different type of work with the hands.

These shape differences reflect the two sources of women's uneven bars. Though the apparatus itself stemmed from parallel bars, the tricks that women do are similar to the ones that men do on their single horizontal bar. On parallel bars, the men mainly swing between the bars with a hand on each bar. On uneven bars, the women rarely touch both bars at the same time. Generally they swing around one bar, gripping it with both hands as men do on the horizontal bar.

Unlike the other events in women's gymnastics, for bars the greatest strength is needed in the upper body—arms, shoulders, abdomen, and back. And the longer the arms and trunk, the more strength the gymnast needs. The farther the center of gravity is from the bar, the more strength is necessary to execute tricks.

Onto the area, which has eight sets of bars, walk

the Elite gymnasts. They all go to the chalk tray, which is a three-foot-wide bowl on a pedestal. Gymnastic chalk provides part of the gym atmosphere; the air is always whiter near the bars.

Tracee slaps her palms into the chalk dust, making a small cloud. Then picks up the plastic spray bottle that hangs from the edge of the chalk tray and squirts her hands to make the chalk adhere. She rubs her hands together and goes to set her bars.

She adjusts the lower bar, setting it closer to the higher bar than where her taller teammates put it. Bars should be set so that when the gymnast swings from the high bar, facing the low bar, she can comfortably pike to wrap her lap around the low bar. This distance must be correct; otherwise, tricks cannot be executed. Sets of bars have regular settings; as with shoes, growing gymnasts are sometimes between sizes.

After setting the low bar, Tracee adjusts the tension on the cables that attach the ends of the rails to the fixtures in the floor. Clips around each pair of cables extending beyond the low bar can be moved. Pushing the clips higher, to where the cables spread, increases the tension.

Meanwhile, the rest of Tracee's group are still at the chalk tray, putting grips over their chalked hands. Grips are handguards with holes for the middle fingers and buckles that fasten around the backs of the wrists. Gymnasts wear grips to lessen the wear on their hands. Working bars causes calluses to develop on the palms. Gymnasts need to take special care of the skin on their hands and to cut off thick calluses, which can cause friction on the bars and tear the skin.

Tearing the skin on the palms is common among female and male gymnasts. The tears are called *rips* because the skin separates, ripping apart.

Why doesn't Tracee use grips? She shrugs and says, "I like to use my hands. Grips would be another thing to worry about. And my hands don't get sore that often." Tracee has never had a rip. This may be because she weighs so little, because she takes good care of her hands, and because her excellent technique puts less strain on her hands.

By the time her teammates have readied their grips, Tracee is standing on her low bar, cleaning chalk off the high bar with a piece of fine sandpaper. She jokes, "It's snowing, it's snowing," as bits of yesterday's chalk float through the air.

Leslie wipes her eyes with the back of her hand and goes to adjust a set of bars near Tracee. When Leslie has her bars set, Tracee hands her the sandpaper to clean off her rails.

Tracee jumps to grab the high bar, swings back and forth, then drops off. She goes to tighten the cables. She pushes up one clip; when she steps to the other side, she finds Amy already pushing up the other clip.

Amy says, "My hands are sore. I'm afraid this one will rip today. Oh, I wish we could skip bars today and go to vaulting right now."

Tracee cocks her head and sighs, then reaches for the low bar. She swings with her knees bent and watches Amy sadly insert a piece of foam into the lower front of her leotard, to absorb the impact when she whips around the low bar, especially if she happens to hit it with her hip bones instead of with the tops of her tensed thigh muscles, the quadriceps.

Amy and many other gymnasts have bruises on the front of their hips.

Amy sets her bars, then readjusts her grips and the piece of foam. Tracee continues swinging on the low bar, her knees and ankles bent so that she hangs in a squatting position. Behind her, Amy calls out, "Who was working these bars? They're even too far apart for me!"

Tracee drops off the low bar and answers, "Some giant," as she walks to the chalk tray. After putting more chalk on her palms, she runs and leaps for the high bar. From it she swings back and forth. At the front of her swing she pikes to wrap her legs under the low bar. At the top of her backswing she lets go for a moment and then regrasps as she drops into her downswing.

Tracee gets the feel of the bars, the feel of swinging. It should look effortless, as if it's done without using any muscle. Gymnasts spend years refining their swing. Given the number of hours Tracee has spent on bars, it is not surprising that she feels so at home swinging on them. She says, "I always liked bars best. I guess it's because I always loved to swing on things—trees, tires, doors, anything. It's fun!"

Bars is the favorite event of many, perhaps most, young gymnasts. The happiest moment in Tracee's life may have been when she discovered a set of homemade bars behind the house of her grandparents. After watching her and Coral playing on the beam, which Coral adored, Big Rip decided to make a set of bars for his younger granddaughter, T.T. Big Rip calls her TNT or Little Dynamite. With the help of a welder who lived on his block, Big Rip made a frame for bars with some old pipes. When the wooden rails he had ordered arrived, he set the bars in concrete in the backyard. Big Rip and Joy spent weekends in their backyard, watching Coral dance on the beam and Tracee swing on the bars.

COMPULSORY BARS

In the gym Tracee warms up her swing, getting into her rhythm and timing. On some swings she wraps her body around the low bar, lets go of the high bar, and sails around the low bar. Her bangs fly and then resettle on her forehead. She jumps off when Dick calls, "Tracee, now run through the compulsory a few times—with full extension and toes pointed all the way through."

Tracee goes to the chalk tray as Leslie leaves it. Tracee rubs chalk between her hands, quickly shakes them over the tray, and runs back to face the low bar. She blows onto her palms to cool them, then drops her arms to her sides and glares at the low bar. Suddenly she tosses her arms back and then forward to leap for the bar. As she grabs, Dick yells, "Form, Tracee . . . and, Jaynie, you've got to keep your feet together. Use the foam."

Jayne drops off and goes to get a small piece of foam. Standing before her low bar, she puts the foam between her heels, then mounts the bar. She continues through the routine with the foam between her feet. When the foam drops, she gets down, reinserts it, and jumps for the bars again. She explains, "I have a tendency to let my feet separate, and that's a deduction every time I do it. So, working bars with this foam between my feet gets me into the habit of keeping my feet together.''

Dick walks over to Tracee and says, "Sickled feet."

Immediately Tracee points her toes straight out. Sickled feet are feet that look like sickles—curved around so that the toes point toward each other like a pair of sickles. Tracee has the bad habit of letting her feet sickle in. At meets judges can deduct from her score for it.

When Tracee goes to chalk up again, Dick asks, "Were you born with sickled feet?"

She laughs and shakes her head. Sickled feet and unpointed toes have been with Tracee for a long, long time. Once, when one too many gymnasts asked why she didn't point her toes, nine-year-old Tracee tried to put an end to such questions by answering, "Oh, I can't point them. See, when I was a little baby I had polio."

On the last set of bars an injured nine-year-old Class II gymnast works out. Her sore ankle is still too weak for practicing any other event, so her hours in the gym are spent on bars. She hangs from the high bar and works the muscles in her arms, shoulders, back, and abdomen. Starting in a straddle pike—legs spread at hip level—she slowly rotates her whole body from her shoulders. She lifts her hips until the insides of her thighs touch her forearms and her head points down. Then she slowly lowers her hips, still holding the straddle pike. Then again she goes up and down, always slowly, with total control.

Dick goes to her, puts his hand on the small of her back, and says, "You've been at it for half an hour.

Why don't you go try your compulsory routine on the bars over the pit—do everything but the dismount. If you fall there, your ankle will be okay, and we won't be using the pit for another twenty minutes or so."

A pit is a huge rectangular box filled with loose bits of foam for cushioned landings. The Academy gym has two pits, one at the end of the vaulting runway and the other under an elevated set of bars.

The young girl with the sore ankle smiles as Dick lifts her from the high bar down to the mat. She hops to the chalk tray and picks up a handful to carry over to the elevated bars over the pit. While she climbs up, Dick calls out after her, "Couple months and you'll be scoring higher than you ever did on bars!"

Many gymnasts become good at bars after an injury to the foot, ankle, or knee, because after such injuries they work out strictly on bars. Karen and Jayne developed their swing and their upper-body strength with a cast on one leg. After Jayne broke her toe she spent several hours a day on bars for months. Ever since then, bars has been her favorite and highest-scoring event. Before breaking her toe she had preferred floor exercises; her background was in ballet.

Jayne started gymnastics because she happened to look through the open Twelfth Street garage door while she and her mother were going downtown during the summer of 1973. Jayne and her mother watched; Jayne thought that since her dance studio was closed for the summer, she could stay in shape for ballet by taking gymnastics lessons until the fall. She never made it back to the ballet studio. And her younger sister, Julie, got hooked on gymnastics too.

When Jayne and Julie wanted to train every day

of the week, their mother, Peggy, tried to explain to her daughters and to Linda and Dick that she could not afford that many classes. Dick responded, "Can you type? Can you answer the phone?"

"I guess so," Peggy replied.

Dick looked straight at her, placed his fists on his hips, and said, "Well, what are you waiting for? You've got a job to do!"

Ever since then, Peggy has held the office together—billing, typing, phoning, selling leotards, writing and duplicating and mailing the monthly newsletter, and coordinating countless details. One job benefit is that she occasionally gets to watch two of her six children doing gymnastics. Another is that her youngest, Tommy, can come to the office after school and watch a small portable TV there until she, Jayne, and Julie are ready to go home.

Sipping a fresh cup of coffee, Dick ends a phone call from a reporter, returns to the bars, frowns, and says, "We're not looking right today. Everybody come off the bars. I want you all to watch Tracee work the free hip to hand."

Everyone drops off and gathers near the cables of Tracee's bars. Dick sips more coffee as Tracee runs back from the chalk tray to stand under the high bar. She looks to Dick for the go-ahead. He lowers his coffee cup and nods.

Tracee breathes in and out a few times, rises up onto her toes, and jumps to catch the high bar. She swings back and then forward, arches to step onto the low bar, and turns so that she stands facing the high bar. She wiggles her grip on the higher bar, changing the angle of her wrists.

*A beautifully extended handstand,
with perfect alignment.*

Now Tracee jumps up and leans forward while casting her legs back and out, her body completely straight. After reaching a high point, her toes swing down and it looks like she will crash her hips into the bar. Just before impact, Tracee rotates her whole body so that her toes drive forward and up, her head back and down. This "circle" around the bar is called a *free hip circle*. It is much more difficult to do than the regular hip circle, in which the body rotates with the thighs against the bar. As Tracee's head swings to the lowest spot, she continues driving her straight body up around into a handstand. She holds the handstand until Dick shouts, "Go!"

Her shoulders move forward as she rotates her body from them. From the toes her straight body falls, swinging her feet downward. Just as her hips near the bar, she whirls backward, spinning around the bar without touching it, going right up into the handstand, and holding it until Dick says to go.

After a half-dozen of these free hip circles into handstands, Dick says, "Good, Tracee. Now, did the rest of you gals notice how she waits to begin her circle and how she shoots right up into that handstand? Continuous tight body. Okay, everybody, chalk up and work five good ones in a row. Think *form* and *tight body*. Remember, this is the set for all the difficult tricks in optionals. Thanks, Tracee, and, believe it or not, you even managed to point your toes!"

Tracee drops off and Dick pats her shoulder before she runs to chalk up. Everyone works the free hip to hand while Dick criticizes.

Tracee whirls around in four perfect circles. On

her fifth, she doesn't drive up hard enough and therefore comes short of the handstand. Down she crashes from the high bar onto the mat, where she rolls over and over until she stops at her notebook. For a few seconds she thinks, then she writes, closes the book, and goes for more chalk.

Amy puts on another pair of grips and massages each of her palms with the opposite thumb. She says, "Oh, does it burn! Feels like they'll rip today for sure."

Leslie adds, "Mine burn too, but we've only got another half-hour on bars."

Karen and Jayne listen while blowing onto their hands. Tracee sighs and says "Wish we were working optionals."

Standing around the chalk tray, they talk until Dick calls, "Ladies, what's the gathering over there? This is a workout! Let's see twenty full routines with good form and no falls. Amy, you're falling today, aren't you? Listen, Amy, get up there over the pit, tell that little girl she's done enough routines, and work your compulsory. I'll make a deal with you: don't fall, and you'll be through after ten routines. But I want to see ten routines in a row without a fall—otherwise, twenty. So do it right and you'll only have to do ten."

Amy nods and goes for a handful of chalk. She hops onto the pit and begins setting the bars wider, to fit her long body. Before she finishes adjusting the cables, Dick calls out, "Amy, don't fall!"

Dick watches Leslie closely, shakes his head, and walks over to the boys' workout area. He picks up a low set of parallel bars, only three feet long and set just inches above the runners. He brings the apparatus back to the uneven-bars area, drops it on the mat, and calls, "Leslie, c'mere!"

From a handstand atop the high bar Leslie swings down and drops off to run to her coach. He points at the short, low parallel bars between them. Leslie reaches for one of the bars and kicks her legs up into a handstand. Dick grabs one of her ankles and says, "I know these bars aren't round like the ones you're used to, but try to extend more through your wrists. Think of that line through your wrists. Experiment a little. Think *extension*. Move your hands around the bar a bit, trying to get your feet higher. . . . Better! Now, push out harder through those shoulders. . . . More! . . . That's it! Okay, now get back up on that high bar and extend fully through every handstand.

"Jaynie, c'mere!"

Leslie runs to chalk up as Jayne kicks into a handstand on the low bars in front of Dick. He pulls her legs higher. Jayne tightens her face and body, struggling to extend herself farther. Dick then has her move her hands around the bar, trying to find the grip in which she can extend most. Finally he lets go of her ankles and says, "All right, Jaynie!" Then he calls out, "Everybody working the full compulsory routine?"

For full routines the gymnasts work in pairs. As one mounts the bars, the other shoves to the center of the rail a round synthetic pad that encircles the lower bar. This pad will cushion the thighs and hips each time the gymnasts wraps around the low bar. After dismounting, the gymnast writes in her notebook while her partner chalks up, resets the bars, and gets ready to mount. The gymnasts sometimes

Tracee in the compulsory
dismount from bars high above
6-foot-tall Dick Mulvihill.

linger at the chalk tray, applying more chalk, wetting their hands, blowing on them, and watching their teammates. Coral Talavera remarked, "In Oregon there were so many other good kids to watch. You can learn how to do something right by watching somebody else do it well."

Valerie Brown likes to watch the Elites on bars. Her family moved from Reno, Nevada, when she was accepted into the Academy's Class II program during the 1979 Easter vacation. Thirty-two-pound Valerie finished first grade in Eugene. Her goal is to be able to extend the way Tracee does, to do what Tracee does.

OPTIONAL BARS

Optional barwork is Tracee's favorite gym activity. Though the Elite gymnasts train on bars for an hour and a half a day, their optional routine lasts only about fifteen seconds—a dozen moves sandwiched between a mount and a dismount.

Optional days begin the same way as compulsory days—setting bars, chalking up, and swinging. Swing is as important to bars as balance is to beam. Both are finely tuned and sensitive to stress.

At every practice, gymnasts spend time warming up their swing, refining their timing to smooth out their motion. Once their swing works easily, they start working the free hip to hand, doing continuous circles around the high bar. In between each series they drop off to chalk up and blow on their overheated palms.

Dick walks over to Leslie and shouts, "Drive it up there! Nice going. Better, Leslie! Ha!"

Leslie drops down and smiles at him while rubbing her hands on her thighs to cool them off.

Dick announces, "Girls, I want you all working *Stalders*."

The *Stalder*, originally a high-bar move, was named for Shep Stalder, the Swiss gymnast who popularized it while winning a Gold Medal for high bar in the 1948 Olympics.

Tracee goes right from her handstand into a *Stalder*, bringing her legs down so that her feet are near the bar in a straddle pike before she begins to swing. At the low point her pike tightens so that her legs and back are on the same plane, parallel to the floor. On the upswing she opens her pike and shoots up into a handstand, holds it for a second, then folds her legs down and circles around in another *Stalder*.

Dick walks along the sides of the bars, advising, "More pike, Jaynie. Amy, you're trying to muscle it; you've got to drive out of that *Stalder* harder if you want to make the handstand. Karen and Leslie, looking good. More *Stalders*, everybody. And, Tracee, start working front-*Stalder*, back-*Stalder*."

Tracee rechalks and gets back onto the low bar, ready to begin. She does the free hip into the handstand, then folds down into a *Stalder*. But, instead of shooting out of it into a handstand at the top, she lets go of the bar! Instantly she turns her hands around and regrasps to swing backward without coming out of her *Stalder* position. To execute this move, the California hop change, requires perfect bar mechanics and excellent hand-eye coordination. Tracee is the first female to use this move; many men use it

Tracee performs a Stalder on uneven bars.

on the horizontal bar. Soon other females will master it.

Jayne and Karen watch Tracee while they rub chalk into their palms behind their grips. Tracee does two more sets with the hop change before jumping off to write in her notebook. While she's running to the chalk tray, Dick says, "Tracee, start working your pirouette."

She nods, quickly chalks up, and mounts the low bar to swing into a handstand on the high bar. At the top she pivots her upside-down body, crossing her hands as she ungrips and regrasps the bar on each half-turn. After a few tries Tracee can rotate a full turn and a half (540°) on the high bar. This is the pirouette in her optional routine; pirouettes over 360° can be awarded an extra tenth for virtuosity.

Mizo walks over to talk with Dick. Then Dick orders, "Everybody off. Tracee, we want to see if you can do two somies in a row—high bar to low bar—right into low bar to a dismount."

Tracee twists her face in disbelief as Dick lifts her up to grab the high bar, facing the low bar. He explains that she should come around in a tight *Stalder* and, just past the low point, let go to rotate backward and grab the low bar between her legs. Then, immediately *Stalder* around the low bar until the end of the upswing, when she should let go and stick a dismount.

Tracee tightens her mouth and widens her eyes. She makes the first somie but cannot get into the *Stalder* on the low bar. Dick reaches under the bar, ready to spot her.

Tracee shoves back her bangs while Dick tells her, "Sooner!" Knowing that she should try to get

California Hop Change. Notice her form and her fingers ready to regrasp.

out of the first somie earlier, Tracee mounts. This time she comes closer to making the second one, landing on her hands and then her knees. The next time, she lands on her knees. She leaps up to mount again.

Dick holds up a hand and says, "Enough, Tracee. Rest awhile. Good work. Okay, who's next? Leslie, set your bars. And remember, I'll be here to spot you through both somies, but try not to kick my poor wiggly nose." He pushes his nose around, and the gymnasts giggle as he continues, "It's only been broken thirty-two times . . . mainly in football, but by a few gymnastic feet too. The doctor put a metal plate inside."

"Gee, it must be rusty in there!" Leslie responds. Dick shrugs, lifts her to the high bar, and stands nearby to spot. Spotting gymnasts on bars is difficult; the apparatus has many parts, and sometimes spotters get kicked in the face or can't catch the gymnast.

Dick Mulvihill has a history of using new tricks and technology. In 1977, '78, '79, and '80 the Academy team won the national team championship, and in '79 Leslie Pyfer became the American champion. However, in order for the Academy gymnasts to do well internationally, they need to improve, to keep up with the other countries' top gymnasts in learning newer, harder tricks.

Both the gymnast and the coach must be creative. One of the most important things for any competing gymnast is the ability to improvise—to keep performing when the planned optional routine cannot continue because of a missed move or a loss of balance.

As a ten-year-old Class I competitor on Mas

Watanabe's team, Tracee once missed a trick that was supposed to take her into a handstand. She continued, making up the rest of the routine. Tracee won the bars event, and at the end of the meet she was given a special award—"Most Original Bars Routine."

The last trick Tracee and her teammates practice is the dismount—the way to get off the bars. Usually the dismount is the most spectacular trick in an optional bars routine; the body flies up above the top bar, twisting and rotating before starting its descent.

After watching a dozen routines, Dick calls out, "Okay, girls, now full routines, making every one of them good and sticking every dismount!" They drop off the bars, rechalk their hands, then return to mount their bars.

Tracee learned to do the *Comaneci*, the dismount Nadia introduced at the '76 Olympics. Off the high bar it is a sole circle (circle with the soles of the feet touching the bar outside the hands) under the bar, followed by a half-twisting backward somie off. Tracee developed a variation of the *Comaneci*. Some people call it the *Talavera*. She explained, "It's just the *Comaneci* with a full!"

The *Talavera* is the *Comaneci* done with one and a half twists instead of half a twist. Tracee's dismount has not reached the official scoring guidebook, the *Code of Points;* the most difficult dismount it scores is the *Comaneci*.

The *Talavera* first came to the attention of the gymnastics world when eleven-year-old Tracee used it in winning the 1978 Junior National Championship. The *International Gymnast* article on the meet commented: "Gymnastics has few heroes, but

A thoughtful moment between routines.

Tracee, who is so young, very extraordinary and ageless in her ability, is, I think, destined to be one. On bars (an event in which she excells) Tracee, despite her age, has *at least* equalled the world class standards."

At least part of Tracee's success comes from her personality, her character. Jimmy Tanaka, a former gymnastics coach at the Air Force Academy, who also teaches judo, aikido, karate, and sky diving, has been following Tracee since he first noticed her at the gym of his friend Mas Watanabe. On a visit to Eugene, Jimmy watched her again and commented, "Tracee is one in a million. That self-motivation! She's a fighter; in Japanese we have a word for it, *Konjo,* that inner drive you see here only in a few blacks, Puerto Ricans, and Mexicans—people like Muhammad Ali and Tracee. Plus, she has technique."

VAULTING

From the bars Tracee heads for the water cooler. Her teammates disappear into the locker room with their grips and come out carrying white vaulting shoes. Tracee vaults in bare feet because "vaulting shoes are just another thing to have to carry and worry about. If you get used to using them, then you need them. This way I never miss them."

Over toward the vaulting runway the gymnasts hop—on their hands! They hop on their hands the way other people hop on their feet. They hop without bending their elbows; the push comes from around the joints—shoulders, wrists, hands, and fingers. This hopping warms up these parts, which will spring the body off the vaulting horse, working complex sets of bone and muscle. The human hand has twenty-seven bones.

At the end of the runway they climb onto an elevated platform. There, a waist-high wooden chalk holder is attached to the wall. Hands pick up the cube of chalk to rub it into the palms. The chalk absorbs perspiration and makes slipping off the top of the vaulting horse much less likely.

At the other end of the runway a pit extends from

the vaulting horse to the back wall. A metal base holds the stuffed leather bolster 120 centimeters (3'11") off the floor. For women the horse is positioned perpendicular to the runway; for men it goes parallel to the runway. Men vault along the length of the vaulting horse; women vault across the apparatus.

Like the balance beam, the vault is a fixed piece of equipment; gymnasts do not adjust it the way they adjust bars. However, gymnasts do position the Reuther board—a vaulting springboard designed by the German manufacturer Richard Reuther. The gymnast moves the board closer to or farther from the vaulting horse, depending upon the vault to be performed, the height and weight of the gymnast, and the skill of the gymnast in the vault to be executed. Generally, the better the vaulter, the farther back the board. And usually, heavier and taller gymnasts move it farther back than do lighter, shorter gymnasts.

Vaulting is the only gymnastics event that does not have compulsory routines. Each vault is basically a mount and a dismount, in less than two seconds. As in diving, prior to the event the performer indicates which officially rated skill she will perform. Scoring combines the rated difficulty and its execution.

Tracee stands at the end of the runway, bends over, chest on knees, and holds her ankles as she breathes deeply. This stretches the backs of her legs, readies her for the fast run toward the vault. Her hands leave chalky ankles when she stands straight and looks down the runway at Dick. He is leaning over the vaulting horse while standing on the mat covering the landing pit. When he sees that everyone is ready, he shouts, "Handspring!"

Tracee inhales and exhales, focuses on the horse, and leans toward it until she breaks into a run. Her hair streams back from her forehead. About ten feet before the horse, Tracee flings back her arms and hurdles, sweeping both feet onto the middle of the board and swinging her arms up as she flies off the board, raising her straight body up, rotating until she soars parallel to the floor, then descends to the horse, hands first.

Tracee's body stays absolutely flat until just before she reaches the horse. Then her wrists bend so that her hands rather than her fingertips will touch down on the vault. Instantly she springs off her hands and fingers so that she flies feet first over the pit, arching up and out to the peak of her flight with her body level, then descending to the mat over the pit.

When she lands, Dick pats her shoulder before she jogs back to the start, where Leslie stands, ready to run on a signal from Dick.

Tracee rechalks at the chalk bin, then stands near the end of the runway, where she practices pushing off an imaginary ceiling—pushing off hard and fast. Into the air she shoves her hands, looking up as she leaps into the air.

When Karen takes off, Tracee knows her turn is next. She folds over, grabs her ankles, and holds her nose between her calves. After Karen returns, Tracee straightens up and awaits the go-ahead.

Dick rubs his chin and announces, "Let's go to the compulsory vault. Warm-up with the half-on."

Immediately the gymnasts begin jumping and

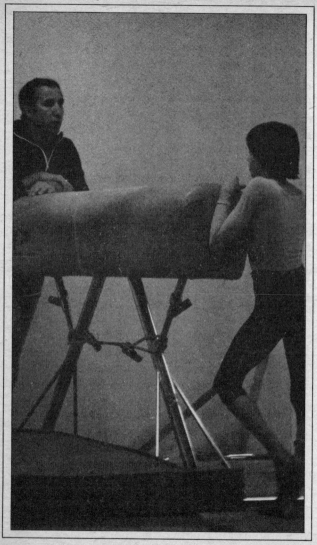

*Tracee and Dick discuss
a vault she just completed.*

jerking themselves around. Each one jumps up and twists halfway around while shooting her arms up. What does this have to do with vaulting?

Everyone stops jerking when Tracee goes to the end of the runway. Her teammates lean against the wall and watch her. She lowers her head, closes her eyes, and leaps into the air, yanking herself around. She steps around to face the vaulting horse and Dick. Up onto her toes she stretches, leaning forward until she explodes down the runway.

Off the board Tracee does the violent jerk! In the air she does a half-twist so that she touches the horse with her body facing the pit. This is the half-on: a half-twist onto the vaulting horse.

After two rounds of the half-on, Tracee and her teammates begin working the compulsory vault, the half-on half-off, which is a half-twist onto the horse and another half-twist off the horse. This is the compulsory vault that international competitors have been performing since the 1976 Olympics. After the 1980 Olympics a new compulsory vault will be instituted.

Tracee and her teammates work the half-on half-off. Each time, Dick makes corrections: "Tighten up, a tighter stomach will give you more lift. Push off harder! Stick it!"

After each round, Dick moves the board a few inches farther from the vaulting horse. The farther back the board rests, the more punch the gymnast needs to sail all the way to the horse. To travel farther requires a faster run, great leg power, and good technique. Although the faster run itself does not count in scoring vaults, it is essential for performing a good vault.

For several turns Dick stands at one end of the vaulting horse, to inspect the hands on the vault, to see whether they push off fast enough, whether the push goes through the wrists and the heels of the hands, then off the palms and down the fingers. The hands must work together, evenly, directly under the shoulders. And the push must be quick. The flight off the horse (afterflight) should be the same height as the flight onto the horse (preflight). Judges deduct tenths if the flights are not of equal height.

When Tracee comes to the end again, Dick shouts, "How many?" She flashes seven fingers. Dick leans over the horse and instructs, "Last three! I want to see these with perfect form. I want to see a fast run, a strong push, a quick touch, a high afterflight. And stick all three. Got it?"

From their end of the runway, the gymnasts nod, jerk into the air on a twist, and shake their legs, while Dick pushes the board still farther from the vaulting horse.

Tracee centers herself on the runway, wipes her forearm across her brow, and leans forward. Standing at the side of the vaulting horse, Dick folds his arms across his chest, ready to look for technical faults.

Tracee rises onto her tiptoes and breaks into a run. As she accelerates down the runway, Dick hollers, "Low into the hurdle! Punch hard! Tight body! Pop it! Stick it! . . . Not bad, Tracee. Only two more."

Tracee goes to chalk up again, then she stretches out the backs of her legs and jerks herself into the air with a twist several times. When it is her turn, Dick waves her on. After she goes, he complains, "Tracee, you're not blocking off that board enough. Get your feet way forward into that block with a totally tight body. It'll give you more lift. Watch.''

Dick walks out from behind the horse and stands in front of it. From the wall he looks down the runway to be certain that Tracee is watching him. He takes two running steps and then sweeps his feet far forward into the ground, with body behind. Quickly he steps back to catch his weight, and asks, "Got it?"

Tracee nods and tries the hurdle a couple of times at her end. The reason for sweeping the feet in low on the hurdle is to maximize height off the board. Like a stone skipped across a lake, the body bounces higher if it comes in lower.

For her last vault Tracee concentrates deeply. Then suddenly she jumps up into a jerking twist. Down again, she lowers her head and concentrates so hard that it looks almost as if she has fallen asleep. Then she breaks into her fastest sprint, accelerating down the runway, arms pumping, knees rising, and feet propelling her body forward toward the board.

Tracee sweeps her feet far forward onto the board, flies way up high toward the horse, and comes down to rebound off and fly off the other side. After she sticks it, Dick reaches over and says, "Nice vault, Tracee. You're done. Next!"

OPTIONAL VAULT

For optional vaulting at meets, gymnasts must perform two different tricks. Most advanced vaults go through the handstand position on the horse; each vault has a ranked level of difficulty.

As the ability of top gymnasts has risen, the difficulty ratings of many vaults have been lowered. Between 1976 and 1978, five vaults worth the maximum 10 points were devalued to 9.2 to 9.6. The compulsory half-on half-off was demoted from 10 to 9.4. Deductions are made from the rating.

Tracee and her teammates compete with optional vaults worth 10. After their optional warm-up of a few handsprings, they begin working more difficult vaults. Once Dick feels they are ready, he shouts, "Fronts!"

Tracee looks down, steadies her concentration, and breathes deeply. The veins on her fists enlarge and she exhales loudly when she looks up and begins leaning forward. She races down toward Dick and the board to punch off into a handspring. Off the horse she grabs her shins, closing her body into a tuck, and rotates around in a front somersault, called the *front*.

Dick spots, touching her back lightly so that she lands standing on the mat over the landing pit. From the landing she falls forward onto her knees and continues rolling to the wall. Dick leans on the end of the horse and advises, "Open up a little earlier, Tracee. You've got plenty of rotation there. Stick the next one."

Now leaning on the other end of the horse, Tracee bobs her head knowingly and then runs back to chalk up. Everyone takes her turn.

Again Tracee readies herself and speeds into the run. Dick waits behind the vault, one hand on the horse and the other free to spot. His lips drawn tight, he rocks back and forth on his feet, and his eyes narrow as Tracee bounds off the board. Up into the air she soars, down toward the horse. He yells, "Pop it!"

On impact the muscles bulge through her shoulders and down her back. Her body pops off the horse as she pushes with her hands. She flies way up in her front (front somersault) and opens just in time to stick it. She raises her hands as if finishing a vault in competition. Dick comments, "That's popping, Tracee! Now, let's get that hurdle quicker and lower so that your preflight will get up as high as your afterflight."

Tracee nods, then skips back to the other end of the runway. There, she rechalks, and stretches out her legs and then her ankles, standing on one foot while rotating the other around its ankle.

She watches her teammates go. After the last one vaults, she steps to the center of the runway and closes her eyes until she hears the last vaulter returning. Then she looks up to Dick. He steps in front of the vaulting horse and rapidly moves his feet far ahead.

Tracee sees that he wants her weight farther back on the hurdle. She takes off, streaking toward the board, and shoves her legs forward to soar way up before reaching the vault and popping off into a front somie. She almost sticks it. When she gets up, Dick puts his arm around her shoulder and gives her a squeeze before she goes back.

At the chalk bin, Tracee and Amy paint white mustaches on each other. Amy dabs on white earrings and then pats shaving cream on Tracee. As Amy vaults, Tracee stands at the end of the runway and wipes the white beard onto the sleeves of her leotard. The white on her sleeves matches the white marks on her hips and her ankles. Her leotard looks tie-dyed.

That evening the leo will be tossed into a plastic laundry basket at the bottom of Tracee's closet. Six leos pile up every week. However, Tracee will not run out of clean leos before she does her wash. She has more than one hundred leotards. She has been given many leos by her teammates as they outgrew them. Tracee loves getting new leos.

Dick hops off the vaulting runway and yanks the mat from the top of the pit. He then wheels two large pieces of machinery over the mats opposite the vault. He climbs back onto the runway to announce, "Okay, gals, I aimed the video camera to tape your hurdles. Now, I want you all working to improve your hurdles. Don't worry about the landing—you'll go right into the pit. Right now I just want those hurdles improved. Okay, Tracee!"

She leans forward and begins her run. Her hair streams back, revealing bits of white from her "shaving cream," but she sees only the board and the vaulting horse. She knows the camera is focused on the board. Onto it she sweeps her feet, punches high onto the horse and up and around, and then, still spinning, she disappears into the pit of foam.

When she crawls out, Dick asks, "How did you feel on the board? You didn't feel yourself blocking much, did you? Go down to the video and replay yourself. See how you did it. See how your arms were late. Harder and faster next time."

Everyone vaults the handspring front into the pit

and then replays herself on the video, watching her own form while Dick calls out his criticisms. After a few vaults, everyone punches off the board faster and lower. For Tracee, who weighs only 74, it is especially important to punch off well.

Vaulting has always been Tracee's weakest event, the one on which she receives her lowest scores. However, Tracee did receive her first 10 for a vault, at the final trials for the World Championships team; she did a handspring front with a half-twist. When she called home to tell her family about that day, her amazed mother asked, "Tracee, did the vaulting judges have seeing-eye dogs?"

Tracee laughed and replied, "Mom! All five judges scored it ten!"

Two days later Tracee went home to spend a few days with her family. On a bike ride home from a nearby swimming pool, she explained her reaction to the score: "I knew I came in with a good hurdle and I knew I popped it good and stuck it good . . . but I never thought they would give it a ten! I don't know how it happened. I'm really lousy at vaulting. *Really!*"

At some workouts Mizo gives technical advice. He retired from competition and got into technical coaching after he broke his back sticking a vault. Occasionally Dick will say, "Hey, Mizo, would you watch these handspring fronts and criticize each vault, going over it on video tape with them? Thanks, Mizo."

Tracee looks from Dick to Mizo and back, waiting for the sign to begin. She shakes her dangling arms to let out the tension. Then she stretches forward, lean-

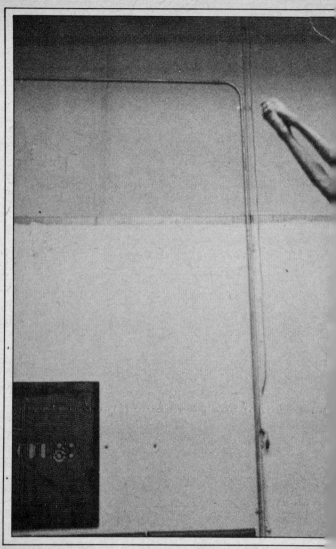

The compulsory vault,
seen from the side in the gym.

ing over until she breaks into a sprint. Up to the board she accelerates, punching hard off the board, flying high, popping off the horse, spinning, and disappearing into the foam.

Then—nothing. From the end of the runway her teammates glare down to the pit. Dick bends over it and hollers, "Tracee!"

Mizo runs from the camera and leaps into the pit just as Tracee shrieks, "I drownded! Ah-ha-ha!"

Mizo yells, "I'll save you!" He wiggles underneath. Loose pieces of foam are flung out and he jumps up, tickling Tracee and yelling, "I'm drownding too! Help!" Down like a dolphin he dives, legs kicking into the air. When he comes up for air, Tracee hurls a piece of foam at him and her teammates yell, "Faker!" from the other end of the runway.

Tracee climbs out and Mizo reaches to grab the base of the vaulting horse and cling to it. He shouts, "An island! I found an island! Nobody life-saved me. I saved myself!"

Mizo leaps out of the pit and runs to the video monitor, where Tracee awaits him. He puts one arm around her, pushes the rewind button, and replays her vault in slow motion. Acting very surprised, he blurts, "What's happening in your hurdle, Tracee? See your feet here? Let's run through in slow motion a few more times. What's wrong with those feet, Tracee?"

She waves a foot between them and the TV monitor, admitting, "Flat feet!"

"Totally flat," agrees Mizo. "And, Tracee, what do flat feet do for a hurdle?"

"Not punch off good?"

"And what will you not have on your next vault, Miss Talavera?"

"Flat feet."

Mizo closes his eyes and then opens them, adding, "And flat feet can cause foot injuries. It's hard for feet to punch off flat. Don't ever run flat or leap flat. It can hurt and it looks ugly—not right for *artistic* gymnastics."

Mizo flutters his eyelashes and begins jumping in the air. He says, "Compare these jumps." He alternates pointing his toes with keeping his ankles bent, and asks, "Which looks better, Tracee? Which gives me the higher lift?"

Tracee rocks from side to side and bites her fingers. Mizo lowers his face to hers. Suddenly he throws his arms out and shouts, "Tracee gets it— she's got it!"

She rolls her eyes and walks off. Mizo laughs and challenges, "If you know *how* to jump, let's see you jump right!"

Tracee kangaroo-hops to the end of the runway, pivots, and bows deeply, smiling until she notices that Mizo is behind the camera, still video-taping her. She shrieks, "Oh, *Mizo!*"

Mizo wasn't always comfortable with Tracee. He remembers when she came to the Academy: "I was coaching the Class Is, who were older. Tracee had just turned eleven and she was so tiny. I was afraid I wouldn't be able to talk with her. And my English wasn't good then. But Tracee is easy to talk to—so intelligent, so strong mentally. I talk to her like an adult, a mature adult. I never met a girl so smart. When you tell her something, she looks right into your eyes and she hears what you say. Most kids listen but they don't hear. Tracee hears . . . and understands."

"Tracee has discipline. She's the only one who never cries. She works very hard but she never gets rattled, no matter what happens. She's calm, even tempered. I think she has more fun in the gym than the other Elites, enjoys it more."

Dick asks, "Is that nineteen? Okay. Only one more vault, so make it your best today. Each one of you could improve. Tracee, looking real good, but remember all Mizo said. Get up there, Leslie, try the last one in pike position. Jaynie, you still have to run faster. Amy, same thing. Karen, your form has improved, but try to close your tuck faster. Now, I want to see all five of you throwing this last vault better. Tracee, you ready?"

WARM-DOWN

Tracee and her teammates warm down by increasing their flexibility. Their muscles have relaxed during more than six hours of use, so this is a good time to increase the range of motion in the joints. More flexibility means better form, finer execution, and less chance of injury.

The gymnasts go to the wall where the horizontal bars are attached. Here, working in pairs, they stretch their splits.

Tracee faces away from the wall and grabs the bars behind her. Standing upright, she raises one leg high in front of her. Leslie reaches up to push the foot still higher and keep it there. When Leslie lets go, Tracee holds her leg up for as long as she can. Then they stretch Tracee's other leg. Her left leg does not go as high as her right; her split is better with her right foot forward than with her left. Then they exchange places so that Tracee can help Leslie stretch.

Next, they stretch the side splits. Standing sideways to the bars, Tracee lifts her outside leg. Leslie pushes it higher. When Leslie lets go, Tracee tries to hold her leg up to the side. Then Tracee turns around and stretches her other leg to the side. After Leslie

Stretching.

135

helps her, they switch places to stretch Leslie's legs to the side.

Last comes stretching the legs backward. Tracee stands a few feet from the bars, facing them and holding one at chest height. Keeping her torso as upright as possible, she lifts one leg backward. Leslie assists by stretching it farther up. This stretches Tracee's back, too; each joint between the vertebrae gets arched. After stretching the other leg, they change places. Leslie, more flexible in the upper back, can keep her torso higher than Tracee can with a full split behind.

There's one Elite gymnast who doesn't do any stretching. Tracee explains, "Amy doesn't have to work flexibility. She's too flexible. But flexibility is hard for someone inflexible like me."

On compulsory days—Tuesdays, Thursdays, and Saturdays—the flexibility exercises last about a half-hour and wrap up the workout. On optional days—Mondays, Wednesdays, and Fridays—the flexibility work goes quicker and leads to weight training.

The weight room is actually a separate building on the parking lot outside the gym. Inside are many weights and rows of weight machines—machines with adjustable weights to resist flexing and extending specific muscles.

Into the weight room each gymnast carries a large file card listing a dozen exercises for her to do. Across the top of the card are listed the optional days of the month. Each gymnast has a lifting program tailored to build up her weaker muscles as well as to improve her over-all strength.

Amy's great flexibility,
seen in the compulsory beam routine.

One exercise for Tracee's legs is heel raises. She steps on a platform under two pads placed one foot apart at shoulder height. Attached to these pads are weights that hold them down at the height and weight adjusted for Tracee.

Slowly Tracee raises her heels and stands on her toes, taking the heavy weight on her shoulders. Gently she lowers her heels back to the platform. Ten times she lifts and lowers the weights by going up onto her toes and down. Above her ankles her body remains still, except for her calves, which bulge as they work. Then she ducks out from under the shoulder pads and quips, "Yuk! That thing made my neck creak!"

She marks her card, then sits on an inclined plane and reaches down to the sides to pick up some dumbbells. She lifts the weights overhead and lowers them ten times, ten repetitions. She marks her card, then goes back for another set of heel raises while her arms relax. After another round with the dumbbells, while her calves relax, she does her third set of ten heel raises. Alternating working lower- and upper-body muscles allows one set to rest while the other set works.

In the heel raises, the shoulder pads seem too far apart for Tracee; they rest on the outside edges of her shoulders. For the regular users of this equipment— football players and weight lifters—the pads rest next to their necks.

The distance between the pads is only one of the design features that need to be altered in adapting the equipment for gymnasts. The designer of the equipment consults with Dick about alterations. Dick, who has coached thousands of athletes in many sports, is

Weight lifting.

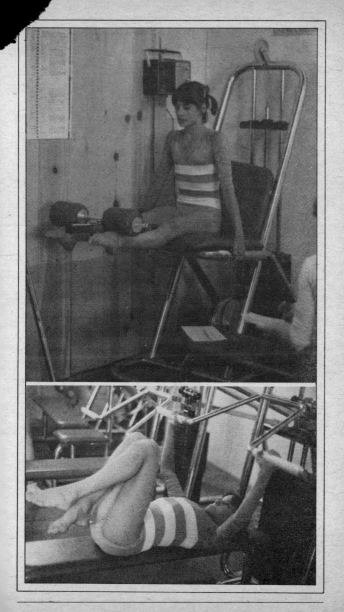

141

always eager to improve the technology of the training equipment used by his gymnasts. The manufacturer plans to begin selling sets of weight-training equipment for gymnasts soon.

During the exercises, perspiration trickles down the faces of the gymnasts, but none of them stops exercising. After each set they quickly mark their file card and read their next exercise.

Doesn't Tracee get tired doing such hard lifting and pushing after a seven-hour workout? "Sometimes I feel a little tired. But, when I do, I just think of the Olympics. I've got a lot of improving to do."

COMPETITION

The goal of Elite training is to improve competitive performance in order to receive higher scores. Tracee trains two thousand hours a year for this purpose. At the end of 1978 the highest scores Tracee had received were 9.65 on bars and 9.75 on beam. In the first round of optionals at the final trials for the 1979 World Championships Tracee scored 10 on vault, 9.9 on bars, 9.8 on beam, and 9.6 on floor. The total, 39.2, is the highest any American has ever achieved in any national or international meet.

Tracee was first noticed outside the gymnastic world on March 11, 1979, the day she won the bars, beam and finished third behind Stella Zakarova and Maxi Gnauck in the American Cup at Madison Square Garden. The next morning's *New York Times* Sports Monday section headlined, "12-Year-Old Steals Gymnastics Show."

A nationwide broadcast began, "Hello again, everyone. This is Howard Cossell, speaking of sports. The United States may be on the verge of producing its own Olga Korbut or Nadia Comaneci. Her name is Tracee Talavera. . . ."

By March 18, after competing in Georgia and

visiting Disney World in Florida, Tracee returned to Oregon. Sitting on the floor of her room with the teddy bear her grandparents sent her after the American Cup, Tracee said. "It'll be weird going back to school tomorrow morning. I haven't been there for two and a half weeks. The American Cup was on TV and in the papers, so now all the kids will know about me. In a way I wish they didn't know. The other seventh graders will treat me differently now."

Right after the American Cup the Hungarian Gymnastics Federation asked the USGF to send Tracee Talavera to the Hungarian Invitational. The USGF director assigned Tracee and Christa Canary as gymnasts, Dick Mulvihill as coach, and Art Maddox as pianist. Christa's passport was lost at the Chicago airport so Dick had to substitute Leslie Pyfer at the last minute.

Competing in the Hungarian Invitational were five Hungarians and two gymnasts each from USA, USSR, Romania, East Germany, Poland, Czechoslovakia, Austria, Spain, Italy, Great Britain, Bulgaria, and Holland. At the meet only one gymnast scratched (dropped out)—Stella Zakarova. Stella was tired and sore; she had won the Moscow News meet the week before and the American Cup less than a month before.

Few Hungarians know English. Meet instructions were in three languages—Hungarian, French, and German. Tracee says, "I learned some Spanish at home, and Leslie and I had French in school so we helped everybody order in restaurants."

Eva Ovari, a Hungarian, won the meet; Teodora Ungureanu finished second, Tracee seventh and Leslie eighth. Tracee found the meet, "Fun! I especially liked competing with Teodora. She didn't look as good as she did at the Montreal Olympics though."

The day after the Invitational in Pe^cs, Hungary they went to Budapest for a USA-Hungary meet. For this meet the USGF assigned gymnasts in the order of their finish in the January Dial meet. First place Rhonda Schwandt had just had knee surgury. Second place Kathy Johnson was at another meet. Places three through eight were assigned to Christa Canary, Heidi Anderson, Sandy Wirth, Tracee Talavera, Leslie Pyfer, and Jayne Weinstein. For this meet Dick replaced Christa with Amy Machamer.

Heidi and Sandy, and their coach Donna Strauss meet the Oregonians in Budapest after competing in Moscow and Riga, Latvia.

Before the events they visited the Parliament, the Roman aqueduct, and looked over the city spread across the Danube. Tracee remarked, "I'd never been out of the USA before so I didn't know what to expect. Budapest is big, much bigger than San Francisco, more like New York City. And, the Hungarians drive tiny cars; they scoot around fast, like bumper cars in an amusement park. They look like toy cars."

The American team was really up for this meet. In international meets the USA and Hungary usually score close but the USA had never outpointed Hungary.

On the first day compulsories, Amy took second place behind Eva Ovari. To many the scoring did not seem fair. As Tracee described it, "We were all getting ripped on scores. But at meets the gymnast cannot protest. Only the coach can object and the judges don't have to honor the protest.

"After Jayne's compulsory beam was scored Dick went to the judges table. He told them he wanted her score raised. He told them that if they didn't raise it he would pull the whole team out of the meet right then. Her score went up a tenth."

The next day (Friday the 13th) was optionals, and the American team suffered. In the first event, vaulting, everything went all right until Jayne attempted a Tsukahara—a vault she hits regularly in the Academy gym. On the run her timing was off, she punched off the board on one foot, tried to pop off the vaulting horse at an angle but her hands slipped and she fell onto her neck. She didn't move. She was put on a stretcher, carried to an ambulance and rushed to a hospital.

Before the sirens died down, before anyone knew how seriously Jayne was injured, the meet continued. On beam and bars three of the Americans blew their routines, scoring below 9. Only two Americans performed well. Leslie scored 9.45 and 9.5. Tracee hit both events for 9.65.

The next day a Budapest paper featured a photo captioned, "US Gymnast Tracee Talavera doing an exercise in Budapest on Friday." The picture, taken less than an hour after her teammate's accident, shows Tracee on beam—the clutch event under ordinary circumstances. The article states, "There was no doubt that twelve-year-old Tracee Talavera has become the pet of the Hungarian spectators."

Later that night a Budapest hospital neurologist

told the Americans that Jayne was lucky. She said that Jayne's neck was sprained. She had come close to breaking her neck which might have paralyzed her from the neck down. Jayne decided never to do gymnastics on any Friday the 13th.

In Budapest they went shopping. Tracee had many boni left; boni are coupons given foreigners in exchange for dollars. She also had most of the expense money the Hungarians had given to each competitor. She bought two small sculptures for her parents and then spent most of her boni on an embroidered blouse for her sister Coral.

They left in the morning for the flight home. Jayne was propped up as comfortably as possible. The stewardesses served cinnamon rolls with beverages. Everyone was hungry so they ate the rolls, everyone but Tracee. She stayed hungry; she does not break her "no sweets" rule.

Two weeks later the Academy team flew to Chicago for a meet. Two weeks after that Tracee, Leslie, Amy, Jayne, Dick and Art flew to Dayton, back to the midwest for the National Championship, this time with Linda and Donijo. When they changed planes in San Francisco, Tracee's mother and grandmother were at the airport to see Tracee; they had a ten-minute visit.

In Dayton Tracee woke about nine o'clock and called room service to order breakfast for herself and her roommate, Jayne. (Jayne dropped out of the meet after compulsories; her neck and back hurt too much.)

Tracee remembers, "I had to be careful! I didn't want to spill anything on my favorite leotard, a shiny

Third place in the All-Around, Tracee waves when her name is announced. Next to her in fourth place, Kathy Johnson, the 1978 National Champion. On the other side second place Christa Canary and the new 1979 National Champion, Leslie Pyfer.

coral one, like my sister Coral! It has two black stripes around my torso. For finals I always wear my favorite leo, the newest one that I really, really like. I think that if you think you look good your routines will look better.

"Sometimes I dream about events. It feels great to dream you do well, and lousy to dream you don't. But, either way, when you wake up you've got to go do it. In Dayton I didn't dream at all."

Warm-up for the women finalists began at 11 A.M. By then the 19 finalists were stretching out on the mats under the supervision of their coaches. Some, such as Amy Machamer and Marcia Frederick, only had to prepare for one event. Leslie Pyfer, the new national champion, was in four finals; she led going into three events, all but bars where she was second, Tracee was in three finals. (In Tracee's fourth optional event, beam, she fell on an easy move. This lowered her score so she was not one of the top eight of the forty-four competitors to qualify for beam finals.)

Unlike the compulsory and optional days of competition, the finals are not a four-ring circus with all events happening at once. For finals events are done in Olympic order—vault, bars, beam, floor.

After the vaulting finals, the announcer shouts, "Here are the girls who will be competing in the National Championship for the Uneven Bars . . . Gymnasts, please march to your events."

Tracee jumps into her warm-up pants, folds over the waist band so she won't trip over the cuffs, slips her arms into the jacket sleeves and runs to join the marchers. After her toddles Donijo shrieking, "Acee! Acee!"

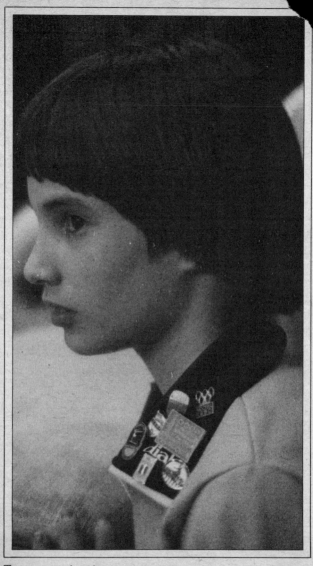

Tracee watches her competitors perform.

The eight competitors line up before the bars judges, salute them and stand still until the announcer says, "There will now be a four and a half minute warm-up period."

At this, the eight strip off their warm-ups, toss them to the sidelines, rub their hands in the chalk tray, readjust their grips and rub their palms together.

One by one, each takes her half minute turn, adjusts the bars with her coach, jumps up to work tricks, trying to even out swing and rhythm. The coach assists, talks to her. The other gymnasts stand by, leaning on the cables, clenching and unclenching next to tense coaches. They rub in more chalk, check their grips, blow on their hands. At the end of the brief warm-up they all move to the sidelines.

Order in the finals depends on the draw. Tracee is sixth; third is Marcia Frederick. Marcia, the subject of much pre-meet publicity, is the first American female to win a gold medal in a World Gymnastic Championship—on bars.

When Marcia's name is called some spectators rush down the aisles to get a closer view of her routine. When the judge waves her on a hush comes over the crowd; human noises are replaced by the sound of movie cameras rolling.

Fifteen seconds later the crowd erupts with applause on her dismount. The clapping turns to cheers when 9.9 is flashed. The announcer reminds the audience that "it's possible for a gymnast to get the highest score today and yet not win because she does not have the highest score from the last two days."

On the sidelines Dick and Tracee wait. They

know she only needs a 9.7 to tie Marcia. Tracee's toes curl upward and she sucks in her upper lip. After two more gymnasts there is another quiet moment when the announcer blasts, "Up next is Tracee Talavera. She is leading so far in the uneven bars. She is twelve years old. Sixth in the Dial meet! First in the 1978 Junior Nationals! Third in the American Cup! TRACEE TALAVERA!"

Dick and Tracee run to set the bars, moving the lower bar in for her. No words are spoken. She looks at Dick and then walks to the edge of the floor exercise area and turns to face the bars. She closes her eyes and releases her fists. Without opening her mouth her tongue sweeps the outsides of her teeth. She remembers, "I was feeling butterflies in my stomach. When the judge waved I ran for it. Once I grabbed the bars I felt good. The bars felt good, they were new ones supplied by the manufacturer for the meet. They didn't bend too much but they were smooth to hold onto. By finals you're used to the set of competition bars.

"I don't think about anything during my routine, just doing it. It's automatic, just a few moves I've worked thousands of times in the gym. Everything that could possibly go wrong already has—many times. You learn to cover them. Actually, meets are not much different than throwing routines in the gym . . . just more tension.

"I was doing a good routine there in the finals. I felt pretty good until the dismount. My balance was a little off so I couldn't stick it, I had to take a step to the side. I knew that would be a deduction but I had to smile for the judges."

It's Tracee's turn now.

Tracee folds down into a straddle pike.

"Tracee Talavera! Beautiful routine!" bellowed the announcer. Tracee recalls, "Then, it seemed like forever until they flashed my score. Dick was standing next to me, watching. When he saw the 9.7 he hugged me. I felt great, like I accomplished something, just good all over."

Right after the meet her former coach, Mas Watanabe who now specializes in youth development compared the two gymnasts who tied for the national championship on bars. The former Japanese high-bar champion commented,

"Tracee needs to refine her swinging technique; it will come with age, maturity. Marcia has a better quality swing than Tracee, more refined. But Tracee has better skills, harder tricks and more interesting combinations than Marcia does."

Newspapers, magazines, and broadcasters repeatedly compare Tracee to Nadia Comaneci. Are they similar? The best person to make any comparison is Carol Stabisevsi, a man who has coached both of them. Carol was coach of the Romanian National team until he defected after playing piano for the Romanian team at the 1976 Olympics. Since then he has played for major American meets and was a coach at the training camps for the USA World Championship team which included Tracee.

Carol says, "There's no comparison between Tracee and Nadia. They're totally different emotionally. However, Tracee is like the second best Romanian, Emilia Eberle who finished second to Nadia in the 1979 European championships, both ahead of all the Russians. Emilia and Tracee have fun and they have similar bodies—tiny but very powerful. But,

Tracee and Marcia shake hands over their first-place tie.

Tracee has more artistic quality than Emilia. And she loves to be watched.''

Although Tracee has a body like Emilia Eberle her shape may change soon. Her father, Rip Talavera warns, "In the next year Tracee's biggest gymnastic challenge may be puberty. Latins mature early. At fourteen my wife and my other daughter had full figures. Did you ever notice that, except for Tracee, the girls who compete for the USA have English, Scandanavian, or German last names? To do well in gymnastics you have to stay skinny. If Tracee starts developing like a Latin her successful days in gymnastics will be over.''

POSTSCRIPT

In the summer of 1979 Jayne Weinstein got relief from the constant pain in her back, neck and shoulders. After months of seeing doctors and specialists, the Asian father of another gymnast gave her three five-minute accupuncture treatments. Within days almost all the pain was gone and Jayne could begin throwing her difficult tricks.

Karen Kelsall also recovered from her injury. Her thighs are now the same size around. She, too, is able to throw all of her routines.

In late summer Amy Machamer flew to Beijing, China to compete in the Friendship Invitational with Chinese, French, Canadian, Romanian and American gymnasts. Amy placed third in the meet, behind Wang Ping and Li Tsuiling.

Upon her return Amy decided to leave the Academy to live with her parents in Lebanon, Oregon, an hour's drive north of Eugene. She stars on the school gymnastic team coached by a former college gymnast. Amy reports, "It's great to have a young coach who can do all the hard tumbling with me. And I like living at home. This way I won't get burned out for college gymnastics. If I kept training seven hours a day I would have to quit the sport totally."

Tracee finished third in the trials for the 1979 World Championship but she was excluded from the final meet because a new FIG regulation states that all participants in World and Olympic championships must reach age 14 during the year of the competition. Tracee will be old enough to qualify for the 1980 Olympic team.

Tracee felt she was discriminated against on the basis of age. "I think that if you're good enough to make the team for your country, you're good enough to compete."

Her coach, Linda Metheny (named World Championship and Olympic coach), noted, "Tracee was invited to be in the judges' pre-meet at the World Championship. This let the international judges see her ability. And during the meet she was able to watch all the top gymnasts without having to perform. Leslie didn't get to see as much because she was warming up and performing. I think it was a very good experience for Tracee, it inspired her."

The Academy Elite group of Jayne, Leslie, Karen and Tracee has been joined by two other gymnasts, Jodi and Julianne. Jodi Lee Kwai, who lives with her mother in Eugene, has been training at the Academy for years. Jodi is a beautiful dancer. Before 1980 Leslie and Jodi quit gymnastics.

Julianne McNamara, a year older than Tracee, came to Oregon in the summer of 1979 from Walnut Creek where she had been coached by Clark Johnson and Coral Talavera. A strong, powerful gymnast, Julianne now lives at the Mulvihill home where she shares a room with Tracee.

In the fall of 1979 the Academy Elites began training early to prepare for the 1980 Olympic trials, and the Olympics. Workouts begin at 6 A.M. and last until 12:30 P.M. Then Tracee, Jodi, Julianne and Karen go to school from 1 to 3. Leslie and Jayne dropped out of high school to train harder.

Tracee has a new floor exercise routine, to music from Snow White. The melody is from the song, "Hi Ho, Hi Ho, it's off to work we go!" On beam Tracee now does a flair—called the Thomas flair or the Talavera flair.

COMPETITIVE
RECORD

1973 Class III local meet, 4th All Around (AA) (7.35 on vault, 6.75 on bars, 5.25 on beam, 5.45 on floor)

1974–1975 Many local Class III and Class II meets.

1976 California Class II Champion, age group 9–11.

Desert Devil Classic, 5th AA, 2nd on bars.

1977 California Class I Champion, Age group 10–11.

California Youth Cup, 3rd AA, Most Original Bar Routine.

Sagebrush Open, 4th AA, 1st on bars, 5th on beam.

Can-Am Youth Invitational, 4th AA.

1978 Region II, Class I, 1st AA, 1st on beam, 2nd on bars, 2nd on vault.

Oregon Class I Meet, 1st AA, age group 12–14.

National Academy vs Japan, 2nd AA, 1st on bars, 2nd on beam, 6th on vault.

Emerald Cup, 1st AA, 1st on bars, 1st on beam.

Western Regional Junior Olympic National Championship, 1st AA, 1st on bars, 1st on beam.

Rose Cup, 1st AA.

Junior Olympic National Championship, 1st AA, 1st on bars, 1st on beam.

Desert Devil Classic, 2nd AA, 2nd on bars, 2nd on floor.

1979   Husky Classic, 3rd AA, 3rd on bars, 3rd on floor.

Far West Invitational, 2nd AA, 1st on beam, 3rd on bars, 3rd on floor.

Kips Invitational, 6th AA, 1st on bars, 3rd on vault, 6th on floor.

Dial Selection Meet, 6th AA.

American Cup, 3rd AA, 1st on bars, 1st on beam.

Mixed Pairs Championship, 5th AA (paired with Phil Cahoy)

Hungarian Invitational, 7th AA, 4th on bars, 4th on beam.

Hungary vs USA, 6th AA.

Western Regional Team Championship, United States Association of Independent Gym Clubs.

Championships of USA, 3rd AA, 1st on bars, 4th on floor, 8th on vault.

National Team Championship, United States Association of Independent Gym Clubs (TT highest scorer.)

Final Trials for US World Championship Team, 3rd AA. (TT scores 10.0 on vault.)

National Sports Festival, 1st AA, 1st on bars, 1st on beam.

Pacific Rim Competition, Honolulu, 2nd AA.

Pacific Rim Competition, Portland, 2nd AA.

Oregon Open (to come)

The Fiesta Bowl, Phoenix, 1st AA

1980 American Cup, 1st AA, 1st on beam, 1st on bars, 1st on floor.

Glossary of Gymnastic Terms

Aerial: Move done in the air; an airborne variation of tricks usually done with hands touching the apparatus.

All-Around or *AA:* Combination of all four events (floor, beam, bars, vault). All-Around score is the sum of a performer's scores. Gymnast with highest AA score wins meet.

Amplitude: Extension of moves. Gymnasts aim to maximize every move, to get the most height, stretch, reach, swing.

Arch: A curved body position with hips forward, arms and legs extended backward.

Artistic Gymnastics: Olympic Gymnastics with six events for men and four for women (floor, beam, bars, vault).

Back: Backward somersault, back somie, back flip; rotating the whole body backward in the air.

Beam or *Balance Beam:* Apparatus; rectangular surface about 16 feet long, almost 4 feet high, and barely 4 inches wide, on which gymnasts dance and tumble. The beam is made of wood with a synthetic covering.

Beatboard or *Springboard:* Apparatus always

used in vaulting, sometimes to mount optional bars or beam; a 3-foot-long inclined board off which the feet spring.

Body Wave: Bending and straightening joints in sequence, making the body move like waves.

Break: A mistake, hesitation, or interruption in flow and continuity. Judges deduct tenths of points for breaks.

Bridge: A backbend; arched body supported by hands and feet.

Cartwheel: Sideways trick, from standing through handstand over to standing; done on one or two hands, or as an aerial.

Choreography: Composition and pattern of moves in a routine; usually refers to floor exercise in relation to music.

Circle: Moving the body around the apparatus; usually refers to tricks on bars.

Code of Points: Official rulebook for scoring gymnastics. Written and published by FIG, International Gymnastics Federation, governing body of the sport internationally.

Compulsory: Routine or vault required in meets. Elite compulsories are revised every four years by the Women's Technical Committee of FIG. Compulsories are designed to include the basic skills on events so that judges and spectators can see the differences among gymnasts.

Continuity: Sequenced moves performed without breaks; a desired smooth-flowing quality; often refers to barwork.

Cover-up: Move gymnast does when something in her optional routine fails so that she cannot continue her planned routine. If done well enough, judges will not detect it.

Difficulty: Skill level of tricks as classified in the FIG rulebook, the *Code of Points.*

Dismount: Way of getting off the bars or beam; or, the last tumbling series in floor exercises.

Double: Double back somersault; double back.

Elite: Top-level competitive gymnast. In the United States there are about forty-five Elite gymnasts. The other levels are Classes I (advanced), II (intermediate), III (beginning).

Exhibition: A gymnastic demonstration done for entertainment rather than for competition; no judging; countries sometimes send their teams on exhibition tours.

Extension: Stretching body parts to their limits.

Fault: Error in executing, in how move is done; faults receive deductions.

Finals: The last section of a meet, after the All-Around has finished. Competitors with the top combined (compulsory plus optional) score in each event compete for the title in that event.

FIG: International Gymnastics Federation, the umbrella organization of the gymnastics associations of over seventy countries. FIG makes rules, publishes the *Code of Points,* and runs the Gymnastic World Championships and the gymnastics part of the Olympic games.

Flexibility: The range of motion in joints—feet, ankles, hips, back, shoulders, neck, wrists, hands.

Flip-Flop or *Back Handspring:* A move; from a standing position the gymnast leans the upper body back and jumps over onto the hands, then springs off the hands and onto the feet; often done in series or to set up major backward tumbling tricks.

Floor: Matted or carpeted area 12-by-12 meters (about 40-by-40 feet) where gymnasts perform floor exercises; spring floors have six thousand springs between layers of plywood under a carpet.

Form: The line the gymnast makes in space.

Front: Forward somersault, forward somie, rotating whole body forward in the air.

Full: Backward somersault with one complete twist.

General Impression: Scoring category for judges to evaluate form, style, and artistic presentation.

Grip: How a gymnast grasps the bars; usually, either regular (upper) with thumbs near each other, or reverse (under) with smallest fingers closest; sometimes mixed (hands crossed). During a bars routine the hands grip, ungrip, and regrip many times.

Grips: A type of glove worn to protect the palms from being torn (ripped) on bars.

Handspring: Springing from the feet onto the hands and over onto the feet; forward or backward (the flip-flop); done on floor, beam, and vault.

Hit: Make a trick or routine, do it well, nail it.

Hurdle: Last step, long and low, before take off from springboard or into tumbling trick.

Kinesthetic Sense: Awareness of the body in space.

Layout: Body position; fully extended in straight line or slightly arched.

Leotard or *leo:* Basic clothing gymnasts wear. In meets they always wear long-sleeved leos, to accentuate the line of their arms and shoulders. Teams compete in matching leos. At meets gymnasts sometimes trade leos. Usually made of synthetic fabric.

Mat: Synthetic cushioning used in all events to prevent injuries or at least to reduce their severity; also reduces strain during many repetitions.

Mount: Way of getting onto bars or beam; or, first tumbling series in floor exercises.

Optionals: Floor, beam, and bars routines all gymnasts perform in competitions; choreographed by gymnast and coach to highlight gymnast's strengths; moves are selected to fit her build, flexibilities, skills, and personality. Gymnast also performs two different optional vaults, ones that she does best.

Pass: A run or tumbling series in one direction, on floor or on beam.

Pike or *Piked:* A body position; legs flexed forward from hips, with knees straight.

Pirouette: A move; vertical stand (on hands or feet) twisting around self; done on floor, beam, bars.

Pose: Position held briefly; done on floor and beam.

Progression: Process of building skills based on fundamentals already mastered; learning moves in sequence.

Punch: A rapid, hard spring off the mat or Reuther board to lift the body high.

Recovery: Regaining balance or swing; usually refers to beam or bars.

Reuther Board: Official beatboard or springboard used for vaulting; developed by a German, Richard Reuther.

Rip: Torn skin or blisters caused by wear on hands (most gymnasts wear grips to protect their hands).

Roll: A move; forward or backward, moving the body around itself, touching the floor or beam.

Roundoff: A tumbling trick. Begins like a cartwheel, into a handstand facing away from the start; from hips, legs pike rapidly, snapping down to the mat. Often followed by a flip-flop. The main way to convert from forward to backward tumbling.

Routine: Choreographed set of moves for the floor, beam, or bars.

Somersault or *Somie* or *Salto* or *Flip:* Moving the body around itself in the air, head over heels; done in all events.

Split: Body position in which legs form a straight line with hips in the middle; legs spread either forward and backward or to the sides of the hips, a lateral or Chinese split.

Spot: Skilled ability of a coach to protect the gymnast from injury; the spotter stands ready to assist by changing the gymnast's motion if an accident seems likely.

Spotting Belt: Specially designed device that buckles around the waist of the gymnast. Attached to the belt are ropes that go over ceiling pulleys and down into the hands of a trained spotter; the spotter can pull the gymnast up.

Stalder: A bars move in which the gymnast circles the bar in a straddle pike; named for the Swiss gymnast Shep Stalder, who introduced the move.

Stick or *Stick It:* To end a trick standing, without stepping or wavering. Judges deduct tenths of points for tricks or dismounts that don't stick.

Straddle: Body position in which legs are spread to the sides.

Swing: A move and a quality. Gymnasts work years to perfect their swing on bars, to get their timing and rhythm.

Trick: A stunt, move, skill.

Tuck: A body position in which hips and knees

are bent, with back rounded, thighs against chest, and hands usually clasping shins.

Twist: A move; turning the body to left or right around itself; half, full, double, or triple twists.

Unevens or *Uneven Parallel Bars:* Apparatus of two synthetic parallel rails kept 2.3 and 1.5 meters (7'6" and 4'11") high. Gymnasts swing on bars, circle bars, change bars, change grips, and do tricks in bars routines.

USGF (United States Gymnastic Federation): National organization that sponsors meets in the United States, publishes *Gymnastic News,* and is part of FIG.

Vault or *Vaulting Horse:* Apparatus; leather bolster held 120 centimeters (3'11") high by a metal support. In competition, female gymnasts do two vaults; the higher score counts.

Video or *Video Camera and Tape:* Means to get an instant replay on a television screen. Used in coaching, to show gymnast what to correct, to see what she just did.

Walkover: A move; from standing into handstand with legs split, over to standing; forward or backward, on floor and beam.

Warm-up Suits: Jacket and slacks gymnasts wear over leos before and after working out and in between events at meets. Keeps muscles warm. Sometimes traded at meets.

Workout: A session of practice in the gym.

ABOUT THE AUTHOR

KAREN FOLGER JACOBS lives in Berkeley, California, where she writes, enjoys her friends and her life. She has been a professional dancer, a school teacher, a child therapist and a consultant for the California Department of Health. She has a Ph.D. in Education. In researching *The Story of a Young Gymnast—Tracee Talavera*, Ms. Jacobs took gymnastics classes six days a week and became a senior citizen in this sport where senior competitions are for those over 24. She became interested in the subject while piloting a boat for a swimming race her athletic club was holding. While she rowed, another club member sat in the stern and humored her. He said that he liked her book *GirlSports* and then asked, "Why don't you write about my granddaughter, Tracee Talavera? She's TNT!"

TEENAGERS FACE LIFE AND LOVE

Choose books filled with fun and adventure, discovery and disenchantment, failure and conquest, triumph and tragedy, life and love.

☐	13359	**THE LATE GREAT ME** Sandra Scoppettone	$1.95
☐	13691	**HOME BEFORE DARK** Sue Ellen Bridgers	$1.75
☐	12501	**PARDON ME, YOU'RE STEPPING ON MY EYEBALL!** Paul Zindel	$1.95
☐	11091	**A HOUSE FOR JONNIE O.** Blossom Elfman	$1.95
☐	14306	**ONE FAT SUMMER** Robert Lipsyte	$1.95
☐	13184	**I KNOW WHY THE CAGED BIRD SINGS** Maya Angelou	$2.25
☐	13013	**ROLL OF THUNDER, HEAR MY CRY** Mildred Taylor	$1.95
☐	12741	**MY DARLING, MY HAMBURGER** Paul Zindel	$1.95
☐	12420	**THE BELL JAR** Sylvia Plath	$2.50
☐	13897	**WHERE THE RED FERN GROWS** Wilson Rawls	$2.25
☐	11829	**CONFESSIONS OF A TEENAGE BABOON** Paul Zindel	$1.95
☐	11838	**OUT OF LOVE** Hilma Wolitzer	$1.50
☐	13352	**SOMETHING FOR JOEY** Richard E. Peck	$1.95
☐	13440	**SUMMER OF MY GERMAN SOLDIER** Bette Greene	$1.95
☐	13693	**WINNING** Robin Brancato	$1.95
☐	13628	**IT'S NOT THE END OF THE WORLD** Judy Blume	$1.95

Bantam Book Catalog

Here's your up-to-the-minute listing of over 1,400 titles by your favorite authors.

This illustrated, large format catalog gives a description of each title. For your convenience, it is divided into categories in fiction and non-fiction—gothics, science fiction, westerns, mysteries, cookbooks, mysticism and occult, biographies, history, family living, health, psychology, art.

So don't delay—take advantage of this special opportunity to increase your reading pleasure.

Just send us your name and address and 50¢ (to help defray postage and handling costs).